BAD SEX,
GOOD LOVE

BAD SEX, GOOD LOVE

CORNELL RICHARDS

To order additional copies of this book, contact:
Xlibris
1-888-795-4274
www.Xlibris.com
Orders@Xlibris.com
740441

CONTENTS

Special Thanks to Marcelle Lofton, James Robinson Jr. who are my two screen play writers for my previous projects, *THE COUGAR CHASER, & CREATING A HOUSEWIFE*. Also to Mariah Pinkney for leading me to Professor Art Danek (Community College of Philadelphia) who confirmed our screen plays were formatted correctly. Thanks a million Christina Welsh, for the awesome festival connect. Great job with Addicted. Special thanks to Rosalind Jackson, Edmonds Entertainment, thank you for your help. Conroy and Chrissy Williams, hope all is well.

DEDICATION

I would like to dedicate this book to **Janet Kay Flucker Haywood**. Thank you kindly Queen for all the discussions and contributions to this project.

ACKNOWLEDGEMENTS

IT FEELS ABSOLUTELY incredible to first acknowledge God for providing me with this talent to pen my third Novella. My parents Altamonte and Beverly Anderson for supporting me to the fullest. My little sister Trish. Janet Flucker Kay Haywood, Dai Meeks, and Carmen London. Thank you again for the tremendous support. Chevelle Howard, Pam Wague, Khaleelah McCleary, for all the encouragement and support. Mrs. Juliet Johnson (Community College of Philadelphia) and Debbie Walcott. My brothers Shawn Richards, Jamahl Browne, Marland Doyle, Lawrence Taylor, Dawud, Maine, (The Best Barbers in the world) Twink, Jamal McCants, Ken and Anthony Bowler. Damien Jones. THANKS A MILLION. Let's Go!

Thanks to my publisher Xlibris for a wonderful job with the cover again and providing me with strategies to get this story in the hands of readers.

CHAPTER 1

Honesty

A T THIS POINT in your life, you may either be geared towards having a serious relationship or content with a casual romance. Nevertheless, I stress that your honesty is vital in the process of finding true love. For those women who constantly place a tremendous amount of emphasis on sexual pleasure as the foundation of their relationship, allow me to probe. What if you met a guy that was extremely handsome, had a wonderful sense of humor, and gave you the world because his financial status was endless, BUT he was the absolute worst lover you've ever had? Again, allow me to stress that this guy's sex performance is critically atrocious and he's UNTEACHABLE. Would you A. Stay in the relationship and secretly receive extraordinary pleasure? B. Stay with your partner and make it work? or C. Leave your significant other and find happiness elsewhere? The level of intimacy in relationships remains a hot topic and according to DivorceHelp360.com, cheating is the cause of 55% of marriages that end in divorce. Although author and researcher, I remain baffled about the amount of women that would stay in a relationship that lacked such a necessity. Or perhaps how many men would continue being faithful if ever having to deal with this challenging perspective. This book is a classic example of weighing the Pros and Cons, and making decisions that could drastically affect your livelihood. If bad sex was indeed a cause for divorce, then the claim would be very interesting. Some would say that irreconcilable differences would be a cop out and selfish, while so called "Realist" would proclaim that life is short and your happiness is more important and this issue would warrant a divorce. Of course there's going to be some women out there that will suggest showing her partner certain techniques that would satisfy her needs but this woman by the name of Stephany Williams is totally unprepared to deal with someone that is a complete handicap in the bedroom.

Stephany was born and raised in the rough streets of South Philadelphia but if you've ever heard of the perfect person? She was close enough. As a child, Stephany won first place at every musical tournament which her favorite instrument was the violin. Being the only African American to contend, her "Spelling Bee" competitors wouldn't bother showing up once her name entered the ballots. She was strongly encouraged to be successful by her father, who was a contractor and her mother who was a science teacher. Stephany is now thirty and a Lab Technician, who works tirelessly at Pennsylvania Hospital and has a bitchy supervisor. On her thirtieth birthday (September 1, st2012) the temperatures were unseasonable and very windy, so she planned on staying home and creating an online dating profile but was called into work at the last minute to cover a shift. Stephany is beautiful. Her mixed features are exceptional. She resembles the grown and sexy, actress Tatyana Ali. Her gorgeous mother, resembled Phylicia Rashad and coincidentally her father resembled Amad Rashad. The agonizing work shift has ended and before Stephany heads home to create her dating profile she's urged by her good friend and colleague Janet Hayes to, "Come on Steph it's your birthday, lets grab a drink." Marcy, who was another close friend and colleague, included herself in the undecided celebration and pressed Stephany submitted. Janet raved and joked, "Wow thirty, you're certainly blessed to be so young and accomplished. Life for me didn't start until I was at least forty." Janet was pushing sixty, very beautiful and had been married for thirty-five years but had recently become a widow when her husband George passed away in his sleep. Marcy interrupted. "She'll be blessed when she gets a man, what woman do you know spends her birthday building a dating a profile?" LOL! Marcy was the blunt type. She wasn't the angry mid- age black woman; she was just a free spirited kind of person with a very spicy vocabulary. "We need to get you some d... Do you want to go to the shaky things men's club?" "Nooo I'm not going there," Steph refused. "Child, don't pay this fool any mind," Janet said. "When God is ready, he will provide you with a good decent man. However instead of searching for the perfect person, you'll probably miss the imperfect person who could make you perfectly happy. And let's be honest, everyone would like for their significant other to have some similarities." Steph replied "Wow, you're right Janet, I mean he doesn't have to be a doctor but successful and with the desire to want more for himself."

All three women ended up just hanging out at a nearby tavern and the irritating gawking began upon their entrance with drinks being sent to their table from a group of loud and obnoxious college guys and one of them taking extreme liking to Janet. However, she instantly shot down the drunken fellow and assured him that she was old enough to be his mother and that she was not a cougar. Marcy tried to vouch for him by mentioning, "Well he was definitely a cutie pie" but Janet just shook her head and continued to sip her Sangria. Another glass of wine and a toast was made to Stephany "finding true love," before all three ladies made an exit. Stephany was doing moderately well financially and lived in a charming one-bedroom apartment. She thought about moving to the suburbs but wanted to remain close to her parents who remained living in the city as well. A few days later, on a rainy day she finally got a chance to start her dating profile. She Googled the top five sites, which were all offering monthly specials. She still found it to be ridiculous that people had to pay to find love regardless of the huge investment that was made during the course of a relationship. Any who, Match.com was selected and now it came time to select her profile picture. She didn't want to appear too serious and pose with her lab coat and perhaps intimidate a possible option but then again if he was intimidated by her profession, then he wasn't the right guy for her. Like most women Stephany wanted someone that was confident. Even if he was a bit arrogant, that was fine, as long as he was not a complete egotistical douchebag. She went with a picture that was taken on the night of her birthday at the bar with Janet and Marcy. Stephany wanted to be unique so she added two extra photos attending an Eagles football game. Although guys would still love a nice looking woman in a dress she wanted to establish a psychological connection by making herself standout from all the other women and showcase her love for sports.

After a couple months of weird conversations and a few prospects tripping over their own lies, Steph began to feel discouraged. She constantly reminisced with her parents about her childhood until the sight of her first place trophies became a torment. While at work, the more Janet told her to be patient, the more it seemed as though her biological clock had begun to tick at rapid speed. Her mother wasn't making things easier with her constant hound for grandchildren.

Stephany wasn't desperate but her father was becoming frantic and reminded her about the original family tradition of having an arranged marriage. "Your mother was supposed to be arranged with this Indian guy but she rebelled and chose me and we've been together for thirty years." But Stephany declined and remained faithful to her 39.99 six-month subscription.

It's now a girl's night out and all three women are relaxing at Steph's apartment. Luckily Janet and Marcy are accompanied by a bottle of Barefoot wine. The Rosa Red blend caused them not to notice Stephany being a terrible hostess. She was constantly checking her phone and even made several visits to her desk top. She finally stopped checking and turned off her cellphone but forgot to do the same for her computer. Minutes later, Marcy heard the signal go off indicating that Stephany had an incoming message. Filled with excitement all three women rushed over to the desktop and saw the strikingly handsome photo of James Pain. Before responding they read his thirst quenching description that boasted about his 6'2, athletically built, 210-pound frame and loved to cook but his profession was Real Estate. It was a bit surprising that at 33 and black, James had no children but an obvious plus. He mentioned although it was pretty rough, he remained a loyal fan of the Philadelphia Eagles. He was also a devoted Christian. That surely rang Janet's bell but there was no surprise that Marcy mentioned, "Ok now let's scroll down to the good part. Let's see how much money he makes. His salary made Stephany look like a well fare recipient. All three women gazed at each other and playfully began fighting and mentioning "he's mine, he's mine." LOL! Stephany finally gathered herself before replying and thanked him for inquiring. They both confirmed being single with Marcy asking about any possible brothers and friends that he might have. Since it was indeed a lady's night Stephany cut her conversation short and promised to pick up where they left off when her nosey girlfriends were not around. The trio finished the wine with Steph smiling ridiculously and possibly creating a little jealousy between her friends.

But there was no jealousy at all, they were happy for her as she would request a meeting on a gorgeous Saturday night after a few more chats with James. He was the owner of a condo in the city. A huge coincidence was her parents were also his tenants. She learned this after finally meeting James and him greeting her with pink roses at

"The Pyramid Club." The gorgeous upscale restaurant was Fifty-Two floors above the city. Stephany looked stunning in her red dress with matching purse and heels. There was never a need to spend hours at the hairdresser due to her unique texture but a few extra strokes of brushing made it perfect. James was just as impressive. He sported a dark gray, Tom Ford suit and smelled like the latest electrifying cologne in a GQ Magazine. They looked amazing together and favored a celebrity couple. Neither was nervous and had a perfect flow while conversing. But Steph blurted, "Ok let's try something different tell me something that you wouldn't normally tell a girl on the first date." Of course he was caught by surprise but answered, "Ok here goes. When I was sixteen I caught crabs from this girl that was twenty-four. I bought some lindane shampoo and when I applied it, hours later it began dripping down my legs along with the dead crabs." "Oh my god that's disgusting. Ok so why did you choose to tell me that story?" He replied while laughing "Because you ordered them for dinner." LOL. He asked "So at the very least you seem to be normal, how come you don't have a boyfriend or hubby?" She smirked and replied, because the majority of men I've met were idiots. It's always the rich ones that are the complete worse. He understood her frustration and accepts the indirect challenge to prove that not all upper class men are the same. She reiterates the same question and he slightly stuttered but replied that being career driven halted or perhaps protected his investment for being successful. His stuttering should have been a red flag but Stephany doesn't dwell on the possibilities of him being dishonest. She's having a wonderful time and she wants him to be relaxed. His true colors will eventually show and boy will they shine as their relationship progress. James was from West Philly and graduated at the top of his class at Temple University. He also remained living amongst the hustle and bustle of the city life in a luxurious condo. They both ordered chocolate cake for desert and at the end of the night he asked to drive her home in his brand new Mercedes but that was a bit too much, especially if she had no intentions of inviting him inside. After giving him a peck on the cheek, she declined and took the bus home. They made plans to have lunch together during the week. When she arrived home safely she just wanted to relax and unwind but a nagging phone call of wanting to know the details of her date came from her parents. They were so excited that their daughter had a great time and was already anticipating meeting their future son in-law. Steph replied, "Can you guys please relax, yes I had a wonderful time but it was only the first date." Her Father said, "If he's an intelligent man within the first forty-five minutes he would have known if you were going to be his wife. Just like I did after meeting your mother and just as the same with President Obama did when meeting Michelle. But we don't have time to chat with you, your mother and I have business to attend, it's our hanky panky night." "Come on Dad that's way too much information." LOL! "Hey sweetie," he says in a serious tone. "I love you," "I love you to Dad." She flipped through the channels and began to watch some late night cartoons and ignored Marcy's call who more than likely wants to know if she slept with James on the first date. On Monday morning while making her rounds Steph bumped into Janet who mentioned that she had a delivery at the security desk. When both ladies approached, the security guard gave her a single rose. Steph had a mediocre smile on her face until the security guard said "Wait there's more" and handed her a box. Inside there was a pair of red bottom stiletto heels. Both women just stood there speechless until Marcy's abruption, "Oh my God these are beautiful. Someone must have given up some booty." Steph jokingly replied, "Well I sure wish I had done so, maybe I would have gotten the dress to go along with them." She then clutched the box and walked away and called James to thank him. He didn't answer but he replied with a text message to confirm she received his lovely gifts.

Hectic days prevented Stephany and James to get together for lunch during the week but they met for happy hour at "PYT" that Friday evening. The restaurant was known for its exotic burgers and contemporary style. They were in the mood for something different so they decided to try some veggie burgers with steamed carrots. It's only been a couple of months with several dates but the sexual tension is overwhelming. Stephany has been doing everything right especially keeping her legs closed until she knows for sure that this relationship will transpire into marriage. James has also been remarkable by restraining himself and not placing so much emphasis on the physical aspects of their relationship. But Stephany's friend Marcy made it clear that her strategy was a complete waste of time and wasn't doing her any good. During their lunch break at work Marcy asked some pretty good questions. "What if you don't like the sex after waiting all that time? What if he's terrible? Are you just going to pick up and leave?" Janet interrupted, "Is that all you think about, maybe you're not getting enough that's why it's always on your mind." LOL! After laughing Steph answered, "You know I'm pretty confident that we'll be alright in that department. I actually went over to his place for the first time last night. His condo is amazing. The wood burning fireplace, open floor plan and spectacular view of the city left my panties completely soaked. First base was enough of a hint that James was a pretty good lover. I felt so relaxed after his soft kisses and the body massage that he gave me after a long day. And of course I felt his excitement but I quickly relaxed him with a massage of my own." Marcy wasn't sold. "I'm warning you that this is a horrible strategy. What if he doesn't like the way that you taste or have sex? Would he be wrong for leaving you? Janet's facial expression was almost in agreeance with Marcy, but encouraged Stephany to do what she thought was best.

CHAPTER 2

Finally

S TEPHANY VISITED JAMES again a few nights later. She didn't give into what Marcy was saying; it was more of temptation that got a hold of her every time James swerved his massive hands into her back with baby oil. He was so attentive but interrupted the pampering with an oven roasted chicken. The Spanish rice and corn was lovely with a glass of Arbor Mist that washed down their food but sprang her hormones. They increased after she removed his clothes, exposing his chiseled frame and alluring erection. He was gentle when removing her robe but she initiated the aggression. It's been a while for Stephany. A year and eighteen days to be exact. Maybe it was her forceful manner or typical nervousness on James's behalf but round one was horrendous. It remained the same for round two and three but Stephany still wasn't convinced about the things Marcy was saying. Steph didn't want to stir Marcy up so she didn't tell about her sexual experiences with James. He was a complete gentleman during their outings. He continued the respectable traditions of pulling out her chair and helping with her coat. Every other week she was getting fresh pink roses delivered at her job which earned him a meeting with her parents. Mr. and Mrs. Williams were thrilled to finally meet him. Mrs. Williams was putting the finishing touches on dinner as the remaining trio sat comfortably in the banana colored living room. Both men conversated about sports with Stephany chiming in with her disappointment about the Eagles 2012 season. Mr. Williams said grace and they all devoured the delicious curry chicken and rice that James mentioned he always seemed to have trouble making. "Hopefully Mrs. Williams would be kind enough and provide me with her secret recipe." Mrs. Williams was stern and replied, "We'll see how it goes James," Stephany added, "Yeah, you tell him mom, we certainly don't want to sharpen his skills so he can cook for other women." LOL!

Her humor landed smoothly as Mr. Williams asked, "So James, Steph tells me you're in the real estate business. How's that working for you?" I'm doing pretty well. I'm actually planning an upgrade for this building. Mr. Williams had a surprise look on his face. Stephany forgot to mention that James was the owner of the building. Mrs. Williams then mentioned "Maybe it wouldn't hurt to provide James with the secret recipe sooner than later." She then refilled his half empty glass of iced tea. James continued, "Thank you, I should be getting the final design proofs from my decorator in the next few weeks." While looking and smiling at Stephany, James said "Since I've already received my upgrade, it's time to spread the love." The meeting was a success. Both parents gave Steph "Two thumbs up" as the lovely couple was heading out the door. While walking back to his car, James began to joke, "Now the pressures really on for a successful relationship because just in case I screw up the recipe, I'll still have your mom to cook for me. LOL! They returned to his place, with the passion fruit scent febreze welcoming them upon hitting the light switch. The way James showed confidence when speaking to her father and gave Mrs. Williams the up most respect while enjoying her curry chicken was a complete turn on for Stephany and she wanted to reward her man. She bathed him thoroughly in the shower and pleased him orally. At 210 pounds, you would think he would have no problem picking her up but he struggled with her petite size. They managed to make it to the bedroom where he fell asleep after a less than average performance.

She gave him a pass because it was extra late and he was tired. But she was completely pissed. She got herself a glass of wine, wrapped her hair and eventually went to sleep. At work, she promised not to mention a word to Marcy but Janet could tell that something was wrong. "What's up kiddo?" Steph immediately confessed. "Marcy was right," "About the sex, what he's not good?" "It's certainly not what I expected." Janet replied with great encouragement, "Give him some time, it's early and you both are still getting to know each other. During my thirty-five years of marriage, at times the sex was so bad I would intentionally try and go to bed early so I wouldn't have to deal with the frustration of his shortcomings. The humor in this ordeal was he finally noticed that he was being duped and began preparing himself for bed extra early. Hahaha, but his love was so good that during a road trip to see my parents in Virginia we saw a younger couple stranded on the side of the road while it was snowing and he pulled over and called road side assistants for the couple and had the services billed to his credit card. They don't make men like that anymore or even people. They just ride on by or walk pass those in genuine need." "You know what Janet you're right, just don't say anything to Marcy I don't want to hear her mouth." "I won't say anything but I think you should be honest and tell her she was correct at least for now." "Damn, you're right again, ok I will." Stephany did just that at the end of the day with a well expected "I told you so" from Marcy." Steph mentioned that she would hang in there with James because he was such a sweet guy and more importantly, she had just introduced him to her parents. Marcy challenged, "You're a better woman than me, I definitely want to see how long this is going to last." James was a sweetheart, that weekend he took Steph on a high end shopping spree at the King of Prussia Mall right before the upcoming Christmas holiday. He even asked her mother's opinion for how the lobby of the condo should be decorated and bought gifts for her parents and purchased a family pack of floor seats to watch the 76ers.

He thought the world of Stephany, it wasn't the money that was spent it was the time cozying up near the fireplace watching old Christmas movies and sipping hot chocolate. She felt safe in his big strong arms. His candle light dinners and sweet soothing voice when discussing his plans for the future and wanting more for himself was pure gold. During this time Stephany tried to fool herself by thinking maybe sex wasn't important to her. She had a decent man and was going to try and do everything correctly and not place so much emphasis on sex. But because James was so romantic at times and he would be the aggressor. Quite mystifying she thought, "How is it that he initiates sex and not be good at it." That's when it clicked, the reason why James was single. But she spared him the embarrassment and just focused on all the wonderful things that he brought to the table, like the enormous respect that he had for her. As things moved forward he began asking for her opinion on business deals. All the boring things some women take for granted when faced with the obstacle of not being pleased physically. For the New Year's celebration, James wanted to have a small get together at his condo. He wanted to introduce Stephany to his parents Mr. and Mrs. Pain. Her parents were invited along with Janet and Marcy which both women thought James was adorable and was instantly captivated by his luxurious condo. His parents thought she was just as sweet as maple

CORNELL RICHARDS

syrup with Marcy whispering "Oooh girl look at this balcony, I would certainly be a bad girl up here. And look at this living room, who needs sex when you have a fireplace like that and a bottle of whatever." LOL. This woman was crazy!

James made sure that everyone's glass was full before he made a toast, "I would like to thank everyone for coming and to let you all know that I've been the luckiest man on earth since this Goddess came into my life and I would like for it to remain that way." Her girlfriends were snickering because they knew Steph thought otherwise. The clock struck twelve and the entire building erupted "Happy New Year." James didn't chat much with Janet and Marcy, he spent more time getting to know her parents and spoke about the great upgrades that he planned on doing for the building. But as the night went on Marcy had a little too much to drink and almost spilled the beans about Stephany not being happy in the bedroom. "Some surprises in relationships are good and some are bad." The entire room was confused about that awkward comment but Steph just gave Marcy a hard nudge and asked if anyone wanted more wine. In the upcoming week James took Mrs. Williams advice and came up with a beautiful garden like theme for the lobby area and new almond color carpet for the condo. James also added a lounge room for the tenants to have family gatherings and events. He had become a very popular young man amongst his colleagues and invited Steph to the most fashionable events in the city. Everyone knew who she was, thanks to James. Whenever she entered the high end stores in the city she was given items for free or blessed with a generous discount. For the next several months the sex was completely poor and very disheartening. Still being mindful of his ego, she questioned him about the amount of stress from work and even herself, "Maybe you're not attracted to me anymore," "Don't be ridiculous" he replied and tried to distract her with talks of new business deals and security for their future.

As his popularity grew, so did his feelings for Stephany and he decided to compensate those emotions since the future was looking so bright. One morning he drove her to work. After pulling into the parking lot, He stared at her for a few seconds and asked "Do you love and believe in me? She replied "Of course I love and believe in you." "Ok if you love and believe in me then go into your job and tell your boss that today will be your last day working and come with me to live the good life. There's no need to give a two weeks noticed because with your love and support, I can assure you that you will not be returning to work here. So basically I'm asking you to be my wife." Daammmn!! She was completely stunned out of her mind but even more floored when he revealed the diamond ring he had imported from Africa. Still flabbergasted she accepted and slowly walked into her job ignoring everyone that said good morning. She immediately found Janet in the locker room and told her what had just taken place. "James just proposed to me and he wants me to quit my job today and live with him. He's outside waiting for me to return." Janet looked outside and immediately offered some of her jewels. "You can't start the next chapter if you keep reading the last. It's unexpected but that's how God works. This man loves you, don't let one department ruin the entire organization." Marcy entered the room, "Woooo look at the size of that ring." Steph told her what happened but Marcy was totally against it. "Ok, now this is going too far. Dating is one thing but now you're going to extend your unhappiness into marriage?" Stephany replied, "Well I can always use a dildo or one of my other explicitly phallic toys." Janet shook her head and mentioned, "No you cannot use the dildo because the problem of him not having good sex will still exist. If you use the dildo, it's in the form of cheating and deceives your partner that he is fulfilling your needs. If you were to leave James because of this issue then that's fine, because you honestly chose to wash your hands, but using the dildo would still be dishonest, it's just on different levels of cheating."

Marcy disagreed with Janet and Stephany nodded her head indicating the same. Stephany then bravely walked into her supervisor's office and told him to kiss her ass.

CHAPTER 3

New Property

JAMES AND STEPH decided to have a small wedding ceremony with close family and friends at his parent's church. Steph's "Vera Wang" dress was supported by Janet who was a gorgeous maid of honor. Of course Marcy wasn't on bored with the marriage but still showed support and was lucky enough to be the one who caught the bouquet but gave it to another bride's maid. The food was a mixture of both Indian and American cuisine with James respectfully mentioning how much of a great teacher Mrs. Williams was and the exceptional job she did with the curry chicken. He also mentioned that he felt like a big kid and he'd won the biggest prize in the world, so to celebrate he would be taking his Queen to Disney World. A romantic getaway to the islands would have been the traditional destination but Steph and James worked hard and they thought it was time to loosen up and have some fun. With Steph's new lifestyle pending, there would be plenty of time to be romantic. Upon arriving safely, Steph called to check in on their parents who couldn't be happier for the both of them. During the week stay in Orlando, the newlyweds had a blast taking and posting pictures on Facebook. Mickey and Mini Mouse were also featured in a few photos along with some frosting from the funnel cake on James's face. Steph loved the fact that James had a big kid personality. One early morning while sipping some tea on the balcony, she reflected on the handful of younger women she encountered who didn't care for sex being a primary concern in their relationship. Steph knew that some twenty plus year olds were more mature and realized the true value of a relationship, regardless if the sex was trash. On the other hand, there were some women young or old and getting good sex but the bills weren't being paid and they were being physically abused by their significant other.

As her sexual prime neared, progression had become a concern and James had clearly made an early exit of his glory days. If he was terrible now at thirty-four, how would he perform in his forties? As James continued to sleep in on the fourth day of their honeymoon, Steph started to read a romance novel that took place in Seattle. It was a story where vapid assholes, passive aggressiveness, & obsessive narcissism collided. It was a modern look at love and happiness told through the eyes of two people who haven't been very successful with either. After a couple chapters James awoke and just wanted to conversate and Steph was all ears. He knew something was bothering her so he entered the balcony and confessed. "Look I know I'm not the best lover but I truly appreciate you accepting me for who I am and sacrificing your happiness and giving me the opportunity to be a great man because I need you." He admitted that he spoiled his former girlfriends with gifts to fill the void but Steph was the only one that stayed the longest. His explanation was valid and better than another dreadful moment. But this was supposed to be a special time and James wasn't even trying to make an effort to satisfy his new bride. She replied nothing but wrapped her arms around him with a kiss that spoke volumes and just laid her head on his chest. He felt just as safe with her as she did with him. What a great sign of relief now that his biggest flaw was addressed. They spent the remaining few days of their honeymoon dining out and enjoying the scenery. When they finally returned home James hired some professional movers to pack all her necessities and she immediately moved in with him. But it wasn't long until he asked "So babe, what type of home would you be interested in living in?" She wasn't sure so he gave her an assignment to start watching HGTV. The addictive network had a roster of shows that aired houses that either needed a total renovation in order to have a dream home or was already turnkey ready.

Uncertainty, turned into total confusion. Stephany knew that it was ultimately their decision on what type of house to choose but she invited all the ladies for a sleep over to help her make a better decision. While watching "Property Brothers" Mrs. Williams, Mrs. Pain and Janet loved the southern look with a huge porch. Marcy and Steph preferred a modern look which "Flip or Flop" catered to a much younger audience. "Love it, or List it" was pretty good and all were amused about the interesting way of life on the show "Tiny Houses." After a month of Steph being indecisive James mentioned "Why don't we move to the suburbs and find a house that's not quite ready so we can put our personal touches on the property?" Happily relieved about his expertise, she replied "That sounds like a wonderful idea." James then added, "It certainly makes more sense to have my parents take over my condo so that they would be closer to my amazing in-laws." It took only a couple of weeks for them to find the home of their dreams located in the New Town Square section. James made an offer of 750,000 which the house was listed for 775,000 and his offer was accepted after he specified that he was paying all cash. WOW!! The five-bedroom residential home had three bathrooms, a pool, barbeque area, fireplace, open floor plan, which was perfect for entertaining and a finish basement. James immediately demanded for the kitchen to be upgraded with stainless steel appliances and a center island so he'd have plenty of prep space to cook. Steph wanted a Jacuzzi and a stand up shower in the bathroom and James made one more suggestion which was to transform one of the rooms into his home office. Their home was fantastic and everyone agreed that they certainly got way more for their dollar by moving outside the city.

It took approximately four weeks to complete the upgrades and their contractor, a small Hispanic fellow by the name of Angelo had some great news. "James you had a budget of fifty thousand dollars but it didn't cost that much, so you now have a remaining balance of twenty thousand dollars." The contractor then gave him three options. "With that money you could either take Stephany on another shopping spree," which she sure loved the sound of that. LOL! "Add a patio room to avoid being eaten by the bugs in the summertime or add a mini basketball court for your future kids?" James replied, "Hmmm… tough decision," Steph blurted "No it's not" with everyone being amused. A shopping spree was the last thing Stephany needed. Since the finished basement was also going to be a play room if they had any kids, adding the patio room for their entire family and friends was the better option. It's safe to say that James was doing Ok, but he wanted better for everyone. While relaxing in his master bedroom he received a phone call from his mother in-law displaying her integrity. "James I think there's a problem with our rent. I tried to pay the rent and the concierge told me that it's already paid." James laughed then replied, "My apologies Mrs. Williams, it must have slipped my mind to inform you that as long as you live in my building you and your husband will never have to pay rent again. So save your money and go on a nice vacation." Mrs. Williams began to sob but of course tears of joy because during this time there was a huge teacher layoff running rapid in the public school system.

Stephany was speechless when her mother told her what James had done, but she was more silent after his derisory display of affection on the nights it was mostly needed. It's been a few months after they moved into the house and James began to slack off with sending flowers to her job and cooking. Even his conversations had been eroded. But she didn't address the issue she just carefully observed him and took note of all the things that he stopped doing that kept her around. But on one particular day after he awoke from an evening nap she complained about his irregular sleeping habits. He argued that "Sometimes you don't have to be an early bird to catch the worm, as long as the job gets done." He then posted on Facebook asking his 1,700 plus friends if they had to choose an hour of the day to wake up for the rest of their lives which time would it be?" Almost half replied with answers stating "Some part of the early morning." He continued and mumbled "What part of living the good life didn't you understand?" Steph remained quiet and just walked away. Janet and Marcy occasionally visited but for the most part Steph had become a lonely queen living in a palace. Steph remembered Janet mentioning "Giving James some time because they were still getting to know each other," and Steph was confident that things would eventually come full circle, that's why she married James. But for the next several months the sex was abysmal. He was more consumed with work and less interested in how she spent her days. Steph went from feeling productive with having a career doing lab work that could possibly help people, if a cure was ever to be discovered for fatal a disease, to now feeling like a lab experiment. The marriage didn't feel real to her, and they quickly became emotionally detached. The house, honeymoon, the shopping sprees, felt like she had won the Super Bowl but never received the Lombardi Trophy.

James was a complete utter disgrace in the bedroom but he managed to give her mind multiple orgasms. While listening to the classic "12 Play" album from R. Kelly, he remembered a teaching from his father, "Son if you can first make a woman's mind climax, then you'll have control of her entire body." Perfecting that strategy by having charm and wit was a huge contribution to him winning over Stephany. But James was losing that control and her mind was drifting. Drifting into the unknown, the most dangerous place for a person that is single and certainly most treacherous for a married woman. She had bitten off more than she could chew with this issue and quite frankly didn't care if it was less significant to anyone else, specifically her parents and Janet. The thought of calling her supervisor and apologizing had crossed her mind but she just wanted a better way to occupy her time throughout the day, while the overachieving workaholic spent his day plotting on the next closing deal. But this wasn't a science project, so what better way to occupy your time then to get in shape and live a healthier lifestyle. Steph created a day planner that included an early morning run, a light breakfast and trips into town to have lunch with Janet and Marcy. Both ladies were always happy to see her with Marcy being sarcastic. "Glad to see you're sticking in there. Looks like someone decided to use the dildo after all." Steph replied with a grin but her feelings were obviously bruised.

It was now the spring of 2013, and Steph would also hang out with her mother in-law just to form a tighter relationship and receive some tips from her successful marriage which was also thirty years. Mrs. Pain had a very interesting choice of words. "Stephany you truly are a special girl. I know my James can be one hard nut." Stephany smiled and said, "Yeah that's pretty much James alright," then slurped on her raspberry slushy to prevent herself from laughing. Mrs. Pain continued, "Very strange, because he gave me know pain at birth and he came so quickly."

Stephany was in seconds of throwing James under the bus and asking his mother what should be done in this circumstance but she just keep her mouth shut. It's safe to assume that at his age, James would be a little embarrassed to get sex tips from either of his parents. Although Mrs. Pain had a more "Tell it like it is mentality," Steph just simply wanted to enjoy her company. Steph made sure to pencil in their lunch dates for twice a week but eventually found herself returning back to the city for more than just lunch with her mother in-law.

It's a gorgeous seventy-degree day, but not as gorgeous as Stephany who looks like a model from a J Crew catalogue. Her yellow sun dress is stunning and her designer shades were supposed to shun the fools who were bold enough to seek her attention, but one particular character knows her quite well. "Hey, hey beautiful," Steph ignored the cat call. The voice then turned demanding. "Sweet licks I'm talking to you." Sweet licks? Only a nickname that could come from one source and what finally got Stephany's attention. She turned around with complete surprise and was horrifically shamed when Roy Sanders stood in front of her grinning and exposing the most urgent need for dental care. He's a black man in his mid-thirties whose hair needed to be cut along with his shabby beard. He was sweating like a pig and there was no need for him to reintroduce himself. This man was very unattractive, held odd jobs, and lived in a one-bedroom apartment in North Philly, which was a tougher part of the city. She kept him a secret because the man is completely hideous. There was no graphic comparison between him and James physically or financially but sexually, Roy was the best lover Stephany has ever had. He gave her the nickname "Sweet Licks" because he always used her favorite kind of candy which was "Tropical Starburst" while licking her clitoris. Whenever she visited him, there was never a concern of him not being erected or having premature ejaculation. Roy was a wild beast in the bedroom. He constantly plunged his manhood into her rib cage and flipped her around while wrapping her long silky hair around his hands and repeatedly thrusted her from the back. Roy's underachieving slackness worked tremendously in his favor because Stephany would spend her lunch breaks at his place.

But similar to James, Roy was soft spoken and sincere. He was just ugly. He reminisced on how they first met when she didn't have enough money to buy her lunch and he had just received his hundred dollars in food stamps and paid for her meal. They laughed, as he asked "So who's the lucky guy rocking your world now?" She replied, "Roy I'm married," "Are you happy?" She didn't reply confidently. "It has its ups and downs." He's aggressively flirtatious and states "Oh I remember precisely that you can be a handful. But I enjoyed every minute of it and certainly recall how your juices taste." If she could snap her fingers like a genie, they would instantly be back at his roach infested apartment. She almost fell into his arms before he mentioned that the reason for him being in town was to buy some new clothes. "I have an interview for a janitorial position with a company that has a great union. It's tomorrow morning, would you mind helping me choose a nice affordable suit?" This was wrong on all levels. Steph could have easily been seen, but by the looks of this guy no one on earth would ever believe that they were together. LOL!! She looked at her watch and glanced around for any familiar faces and replied "Congrats on the interview Roy, sure I'll help you find a suit." He mentioned that he had only three hundred dollars to spend but she insisted that he rent an expensive suit for one hundred dollars and keep the remaining two hundred in his pocket. A strategy James used to make the best impression without going broke and eventually beating out his competitors. So they got a very nice suit from "The Men's Wearhouse" but a complete make over was necessary. She accompanied him to a nearby barbershop that also had a nailory and got him a manicure and pedicure. Roy felt like a new man. He instantly went from being repulsive to having the looks of a recovering drug abuser. This was certainly more tolerable as long as he didn't smile. But he was confident that he would get the job and then get his teeth fixed. He thanked Stephany repeatedly and said "I would like to see you again but I don't want to interrupt. But I can't call you because I don't have a cell phone at this time. I can only email you. That's how I've been communicating with jobs." "Stephany felt the vibes and said, "Ok you can email me to say hello. It was nice seeing you again Roy." She gave him a much tighter hug with his perspiration odor reminding her of their amorous events. Steph went home that evening with an extra twinkle in her eye and burst in her step, much chipper than usual but totally unnoticed by James.

CHAPTER 4

Good Afternoon

MRS. PAIN ALWAYS looked forward to spending time with Stephany but it was Roy who Steph was looking forward to spending time with. A few days later, the two ladies sat in the park having lunch. Steph checked her email and Roy sent her a picture of him wearing his new suit and confirmed that he had gotten the job. His plans were to now furniture his apartment and purchase a year supply of roach spray. LOL! She replied "Congrats, you look very handsome," and after lunch, she continued to chat with him. He restored the excitement back into her life. There were no talks of business deals, bad tenants, or money, just plain fun and the thrill of his orgasmic tone when he finally purchased a cell phone. But Roy was careful, he never randomly called Stephany, he only returned her calls. At times she felt bad about her ongoing communication with Roy but for the most part she was highly tempted. Especially when he emailed pictures of himself fresh out of the shower, showing off his masculine frame that he acquired from spending hours at the gym and trying to live a healthier lifestyle, while James was busy cooking every damn thing he saw on television and gaining a staggering amount of weight. It took a couple months for Roy to get his apartment completely furnished, pest controlled, and even got new braces for his teeth. But he was still ugly. LOL! Roy made it clear, "Steph I miss you, as you can see I've never been the best looking guy but I'm actually making some changes in my life and not just talking about it. I can't believe I let you escape. I just wasn't ready for you." Those words placed Stephany back on the pedestal where she belonged instead of her usual "tag along feeling" she had whenever being with James. While relaxing in his freshly decorated pad, Roy sent her some photos of the apartment, which she confirmed his great taste by selecting a black theme and leather couches. But the last photo that Roy sent was of his rock hard, vein bulging penis, covered with a syrup dripping strawberry. The timing of the picture arrived just minutes after James was able to satisfy himself. Terrible!

Stephany and James's marriage was like a thunderstorm but Steph was the only one left out in the trenches. She wasn't given an umbrella or coat to eschew the rain so she sought comfort elsewhere. After dozens of sexual conversations and exchanging emails, she finally decided to pay Roy a visit in the afternoon. This time, instead of the tropical starburst, James used some Nutella when licking her nipples and working his way down to her sweet island of adventure. Roy remained on that island, sucking and slurping until she exploded with the most vigorous climax. After convulsing, she returned the favor by licking the Nutella from his scrotums and enjoyed riding his fully erected pleasure log. Roy had already ordered lunch before she arrived and they sat in bed after round four eating subway sandwiches. Her visits with Roy became frequent as he remained consistent with maintaining her freakish manner. Roy bought her some Jasmine flowers which were kept at his place for obvious reasons. He also out did James when massaging her entire body and rubbing her feet. His kisses were even better because the braces instantly began to adjust his teeth. She felt so relaxed and more at home with Roy but the provoking thought of how to continue keeping him a secret from her girlfriends was troubling. She was insanely glowing whenever around them and when questioned, Steph considered lying that James finally got it together. But Marcy was like a shark and easily smelled the scent of good sex all over her. "What the hell is going on with you?" she asked. "What are you talking about? Steph replied "Come on don't play dumb with me, Janet can't you tell that somethings up with this chick?" "Yup, spill it kiddo" "Ok, ok."

I ran into an old friend, and I've been on cloud twelve ever since." Steph then showed them a picture of Roy. Marcy almost puked. "Oh my God, is that what's been keeping your head in the clouds? You would have been better off using the dildo. Janet take a look at this foolishness."

When Janet saw the photo she was speechless but was more inquisitive and asked "Ok why?"

"Janet his sex is so intoxicating. I know he's not good looking but he has everything a woman could desire in a man. The way he treats me as if I'm the first and only resort, he's made some really great changes and taking care of himself, and oh if I didn't mention it, his sex is phenomenal." She then continued to show Roy's shirtless photos and a few X-rated pics. That certainly caught Marcy's attention as she asked "Oh let me see that one again. Hey at least you cheated at the beginning, most women wouldn't even have gotten this far." But of course Janet was the one to implement the substance. "You fool, there's no reason for cheating at all in the beginning, middle or end of a marriage. But for my own curiosity can I see that second picture again." LOL! Janet continued, "You have to end this, these dealings usually don't end very well, especially when it sounds like you're on the verge of catching feelings for this man." Steph replied, "I know Janet it's just for once since I've been married, I'm finally getting everything I want and need and it's just so hard to let go. I know this sounds silly but my infidelity has certainly saved my marriage. Janet was intrigued with Marcy adding "Please do tell." "Whenever I leave Roy and go home to James, I'm not as irritable, I don't notice being ignored by James, every time he rambles about things that goes on in his business meetings I just sit there and pretend like I'm listening with a smile on my face with thoughts of Roy having no problem licking my ass and enjoying it. I find myself being extra polite to people on the street and very oddly, pretending that I'm with Roy when pleasing my husband until I'm brought back to reality when he comes faster than the express train. I know it sounds horrible but it's the facts of my life at the moment. It's really not that easy for me to leave either one of these men because both brings a special something to my life that every woman deserves. I know that sounds a bit selfish and I agree with you Janet, that this might not end well, but I'm certainly glad to have two supportive friends like you to stick with me and realize that, overall I'm having the time of my life right now."

Marcy asked, "So cheating motivates you to do more for your husband? Janet I thought I was the crazy one. She's lost it. But you're right Steph we're here for you and hoping all goes well." Janet stated, "Well I'm the oldest and theoretically supposed to be the one who went crazy first. But I recently read something in a magazine related to Steph's issue. This psychologist mentioned that, now in this era where the gay and lesbian communities are receiving these historical rights, you rarely, if at all hear about sex issues in their relationships. The majority of these issues are with the heterosexual couples. Similar to their community, heterosexuals have spent millions of dollars trying to enhance physical appearance or trying to detach ourselves from vows that have been turned into bitter revengeful words through divorce. It was a very interesting article." No surprise to Marcy's harsh reply, "The reason why you don't hear about it, is because no one cares and it's disgusting. Steph mentioned, "I understand the concept of that story Janet, you don't have to like their preference but it forces self-reflection and to ask yourself what are they doing correctly to make their love last and what can I learn from their community." "Absolutely, we all can learn something from everyone." Stephany then received a text notification and she's full of joy thinking it's from Roy, but it's only her husband sending a lovely boring text message about how much she means the world to him and hoping she's having a wonderful day. She totally ignored him and sent a text to Roy asking how his day was going?" Marcy then challenged and perhaps was borderline disrespectful by asking, "So old wise one, when do you think you'll be able to take down the photos of your deceased husband and move on in order to rekindle love?" The question hurt Janet and she got up and sadly walked away. "What is wrong with you?" Steph shouted.

"Well she thinks she knows everything and always giving us advice but how come she's not putting herself back out there?" "Maybe because she's still in the grieving process Marcy, did you ever stop and think first before opening your big mouth?" "Well it's been long enough," "Marcy, who the hell do you think you are? Who are you to say when someone should be over the death of their life long partner?" "Well, she was pretty interested in Roy's photos so it's clear that she might need some d… she was married for thirty plus years. So I can understand her now being on a drought." Stephany's reply was very interesting. "You sound absolutely ridiculous; marriage shouldn't be all about the sex." "Wooowww, so I sound ridiculous and you're a complete hypocrite, we make such a great team. LOL! Stephany just sat there ashamed with her hands covering her face. She then tried to make herself feel better by texting her husband and letting him know that he also meant the world to her. Crazy! When the two women finally departed, Steph walked by a hotel and stood at the bus stop where she could over hear a woman complaining about not being able to get lucky in her room. The mid-age woman was beautiful but snobbish and clearly unsatisfied because her needs were not being met. The woman appeared to be talking to a relative or close friend while mentioning, "I just thought things would be better in a hotel, we have a luxurious room and I'm trying to make this work, I just don't know what else to do, I can't take it anymore." Stephany felt the need to jump in and offer a few words of encouragement while still being a hypocrite. "Hey, please stay and fix your marriage, don't leave." Shocked and terribly confused, the woman turned to her and said "I'm just trying to get a hotel room for my dog lucky, woman what's your problem? Hahaha LOL! The hotel manager then came outside and told the woman she could be accommodated but for an additional fee for the small dog.

So it was an emotionally rough day for Stephany but when she got home there was a nice hot bath mixed with rose peddles and a touch of suave oil waiting for her. Another delicious meal was prepared followed by a body rub. But poor James, he still failed. He didn't want to spoil the moment so he didn't initiate sex which Steph was in much need to be touched. As James slept peacefully, anxiety kicked in and she got comfortable and began to please herself on the couch. The love seat was certainly jealous as it was the first time since moving there that the couch had seen that much action. So sad, James even awoke in the middle of her session and hopelessly watched. Although entertaining to a stranger's eye, it was extremely degrading for him to realize that her fingers were far more gratifying than his manhood. He went back to bed in despair but Stephany slept comfortably like a well fed baby. The next morning James sat at the table reading the newspaper. Steph arose and was shocked to see him because he usually left just after sunrise to get a jump start on the day. She had made plans to see Roy in the afternoon but James had a surprise for her. "We have an important meeting today, and I would love to bring you in to have your opinion on a very important business deal." She then tried to talk her way out of it, "Oh come on, you know I'm no good at those things, you're the brains of the operation." But he insisted. "I think you'll be able to handle this one." They both showered and got dress. It was a bit unusual because James was looking more casual and wasn't wearing one of his tailor made suits. "You're wearing jeans and a t-shirt; I thought you said we were making a business deal?" "Just relax honey." Minutes later they pulled into a BMW dealership. Steph immediately was mesmerized by the luxurious vehicles as the salesman who spoke with a heavy Italian accent approached and was glad to see them. "James, James my friend welcome back, is this the Queen? She looks like an angel straight down from heaven. These are the bullshit cars, please, please come in the back

James." In the back of the dealership, the salesman had a brand new i8 and x6 under a cover.

The x6 was cherry red and the i8 was white. The salesman instantly began making his tempting offer. "This is the lifestyle you need Stephany, step inside of this beautiful car, it loves you." It was a gorgeous vehicle. The scissor doors of the BMW i8 provided an undeniable emotional and sporty allure that make it truly one-of-a-kind. "Come Stephany," the salesman ordered, "You need some extra room for your friends and don't want to spend that much, the x6 is perfect for you. This is a beauty." The salesman then turned and asked, "James what do you think?" James replied, "It doesn't matter what I think, it's all about what my beautiful loyal wife thinks. She puts up with a lot from me, that's my sunshine, and I just want to reward her." The salesman then asked "So which one will it be Stephany? She remained confused but chose the i8. "Excellent choice," the salesman shouted. He then tells one of the workers to quickly clean it off and escorted the couple to his office to do the paperwork. "Ok James excellent choice, the vehicle is 145,000 but because you're such a great customer and it's for your lovely wife, I'll give it to you for 120,000. James arrogantly replied "That's not a problem, I'll do you a favor also and save you some paperwork and just write a check for the full amount right now." Stephany's eyes lit up and gazed at the two men wiping down her new car. The salesman then mentioned "Stephany, you're going to own the road with this vehicle, just be careful it's a very fast car." She was so excited and couldn't stop hugging and kissing James. The salesman said "Ok, ok, not in my office, here are the keys and congratulations." It was truly an incredible vehicle and she couldn't wait to show it off to her girlfriends. But first James took it for a spin and they went and visited her parents who were completely blown away. "Wow, you guys are really living the life," Mrs. Williams said, but Mr. Williams asked for a test drive which they allowed him to take it around the block and he joked about picking up a few honeys and not coming back. LOL!

A few days later as Marcy mustered up the courage to finally apologize to Janet, the two women sat in the park restoring their friendship but was interrupted by Steph causing a scene with her sudden approach along with a bit of embarrassment due to having difficulty parking. On-lookers gazed and little children awaited to be pleasantly surprised by who they thought could only be one of their favorite athletes. She wasn't a celebrity but she received the A list treatment when few mistook her for a soap opera star and began posing for pictures. Marcy and Janet just stood in amazement as Stephany played along well and soaked up all the attention. When the excitement ceased, Marcy raved, "That car is spectacular, now I will admit I'm jealous." Janet asked, "Congrats Steph, what kind of car is that? I've never seen anything like it." Steph replied that "It's a new BMW and that James had just surprised me with it this morning. But more importantly I'm glad that you both are friends again. The car is a two seater so as a reward for this reconciliation, here are the keys Janet. Take Ms. Crazy for a quick spin. I'll wait right here for you to return." Excited and without hesitation, Janet grabbed the keys and the two left skid marks on the ground with Stephany standing in a cloud of smoke. She knew that they would be a while, Marcy even called to let Steph know that some unexpected errands had come up but there were no worries. Stephany gave them the go ahead, while she spent the next couple of hours sucking on Roy's head and eventually fell asleep. There were two missed phone calls from James, who was just checking in to see if she was having fun. She was actually having a great time after Roy awakened her with his soft kisses and touching her everywhere.

CHAPTER 5

Not Cool

IT'S TOTALLY NATURAL for Roy to have an emotional connection with Stephany but he didn't allow his feelings to cloud his judgment when thinking about the possibilities of a true relationship. But Stephany's emotions were a little over the top. She didn't tell Roy about the new car, she just surprised him at work one day while on his break. She brought him lunch and gave him a big kiss as his boss and co-workers stood with a jaw dropping, disoriented look on their faces. It was now Roy who felt like a star and patted Stephany on the butt after one last smooch with her saying, "I'll call you later" and waving goodbye. He ignored everyone as they continued to stare and grabbed an orange crate and sat in the corner eating his sandwich with a huge smile on his face. This went on for weeks with Roy receiving all the husband benefits, and Stephany forgetting to say "Thank you" whenever James gave her flowers or did something nice for her. She allowed Roy to drive the BMW while her face was often buried in his lap and him ejaculating in her mouth then kissing her husband upon returning home. Disgusting wretch! Her actions were becoming too obvious and suspicions began to surface but James was naive. He thought she was just slacking off due to hanging out with her girlfriends and having fun with the new car. James was a great cook but what great cook prepares food only to dine alone? Stephany's late returns left him at the dinner table by himself with the candles lit but he was nice enough to always leave her dinner in the microwave. Quite often with a love note that read sweet nothings because his words weren't going in one ear and out the other, his words failed to enter since her head remained on cloud twelve due to a constant addiction for Roy.

But a mother knows her daughter the best and it was time for an intervention. Mrs. Williams contacted her daughter to schedule an appointment because she sensed the deception, unfaithfulness and shame that Stephany was bringing down on the family. Instead of a public area, the two beauties sat in the comfort of her parent's home. Mrs. Williams opened very bluntly, "I am unaware of the exact details but something very strong is telling me that you are at tremendous fault of wrong doing." Wrong doing was a feeling that Mrs. Williams knew all too well. Stephany was silent, but with tears flowing which provided the confirmation. She finally replied, "Mom, I'm in a real tough spot right now and have fell out of love with my dashing husband who has treated me like a Queen and provided me with a fairy tale lifestyle." Mrs. Williams asked "So who is this man that is contributing to your confusion?" Stephany showed her the picture of Roy in his work uniform and Mrs. Williams surprisingly said. "I understand the appeal of this man." Uncertain about how to respond, Stephany asked "What do you mean, do you know him?" "No I don't know him but I'm aware of his kind. "He's a better lover than your husband. I'm sadden by your actions young lady but I will not be a hypocrite." Stephany eyes began getting big as golf balls with her face full of anticipation of the next few words coming out of her mother's mouth. "At the beginning of my marriage to your father, I had an affair with a very unattractive man. Your father provided me with everything under the sun except fiery passion in the bedroom. This certain gentleman was charming and we met in a study hall. I'll leave the rest to your imagination. "Oh my God mom, are you serious?" "Listen to me child you might not be as lucky as me?" "Does dad know about this?" "Like I was saying, you might not be as lucky as me because when the gentleman told your father about the affair, your father knew why I did it, and realized that the man was just trying to steal me away from him. Your father forgave me and from that day on he has been a monster in the bedroom. That's how you came about."

"I can't believe what I just heard" "I don't care whether you believe it or not, but you need to end this affair now before this gets out of control. I know it's not easy but please pray and ask God to lead you out of this man's arms and back into your husband's heart. You're actually fortunate that James is a workaholic and doesn't probably have time to investigate you because he trusts you. But when he has some free time on his hands and fully catches the vibe that something doesn't feel right, you'll be making a phone call telling me you need to stay here until you find another place to live. You're also putting your father and me in debt because James will probably force us to move out and we'll have rent to pay, not that we can't afford our own rent but how many son in-laws can afford to provide for his entire family? You're not thinking and clearly being selfish. A matter of fact your father and I would be lucky if you made a phone call telling us you need to return home instead of us getting a phone call from the morgue asking us to come and identify your body because this man caught you cheating and snapped, leaving us with that pain for the rest of our lives. Others will fall because of your foolishness. That's not cool." Stephany rubbed her forehead and agreed with her mother that her infidelity had to end but her actions spoke otherwise. Every time she made an attempt to begin the process of cutting Roy off, he somehow ended up between her legs, and sexing her like he had something to prove. But the proof would certainly surface when James decided to take a few days off from work to relax with his wife.

Normally, Stephany would be busy texting with her friends and tuning James out. It seemed as though maybe she was giving him her undivided attention by not texting but Stephany wasn't communicating with anyone at all which drew suspicion. There were no complaints of any arguments with her parents or girlfriends which were the red flags but James pretended not to notice. He decided to hack her phone and email account. She would still be able to receive them normally but they would also be sent to his phone. One night during dinner he asked, "So how are your parents?" She hasn't seen or spoken to them in about a week but she simply replied "Oh they're fine. I chatted with them yesterday." He knows she's lying but continues to eat the well prepared lamb over yellow rice. Hmm..."What else could she be lying about?" He thought. After dinner Stephany even went to bed early to prevent James from trying to have sex with her. Its ok he wasn't in the mood anyway. He checked his phone and saw Roy's text message mentioning that he can't wait to taste her AGAIN, how beautiful she is, and how he couldn't concentrate while driving the i8 as she performed on him orally. James knew that he had to remain calm but being filled with rage, he picked up the kitchen knife that was used to cut the lamb and quietly entered the room as she slept peacefully and just stood over her with a fierce grip on the knife. His cellphone rang which frightened Stephany out of her sleep and James quickly tucked away the knife. It's her mother asking him, "Is everything alright?" and requesting to speak with Stephany. Before he gave her the phone, James hit the speakerphone button and sat down on the side of the bed and watched Stephany like a hawk. It's a real creepy scene as the full moon peaks through the blinds providing the only light in the pit black room. He grabs hold of the knife again but kept it concealed and contemplated allowing Mrs. Williams to hear the horror of Stephany pleading for her life. They have a great mother daughter relationship so Mrs. Williams is aware of Stephany's actions and chose to keep him in the dark while he paid their rent, so over hearing the gruesome death of her daughter would be appropriate.

Mrs. Williams was relieved to hear Stephany's voice but conformed and exposed all what was bad as James carefully listened. "Stephany I haven't heard from you in almost a week, I was worried and scared to death that James found out about the affair. Stephany please stop this, your friends are also concerned about you. They also tried calling but no answer." Discombobulated, Stephany began lying to her mother, "Something was wrong with my phone, and I've just been a little stressed lately." "Ok honey well have a great night, I love you." "I love you to mom." Those should have been her last words but James gets off the bed and turns on the light. Stephany saw the sharp blade and is scared to death and begins to sob and immediately asks for James's forgiveness. He offered her a few choice words then stormed out of the room. James doesn't want a divorce, that would be considered a gift. He really wants to kill her along with her entire family but he still loves her. He's just really disappointed and hurt by her deceit. There's no reason to contact Roy, James never understood why guys got angry and contacted the other man when finding out their wives were unfaithful. Stephany is clearly the only person in control of her actions and Roy was just being a regular guy. He saw Roy's pictures and it didn't matter what he looked like, the typical woman might say "Well if I'm going to cheat it's certainly going to be with someone that looks better than my man." But James was already thinking about how to resolve this issue because he truly loved his wife. He spent the night in the guest room but with no sleep. Stephany awakened the next morning with a romantic attempt by trying to cook him breakfast and almost set the kitchen on fire.

After using the fire extinguisher on the sausages, James asked "How could you do this to me? What have I done to deserve such harsh treatment?" Stephany then turned from a sweet beautiful hardworking Goddess to a complete ratchet bitch and answered. "It's not about what you did, it's about what you haven't been doing, especially throughout

CORNELL RICHARDS

the course of this marriage to keep your wife happy. My parents are in their sixties and their sex life should not be better than mine." James suggested that maybe she should go and stay with her parents until they straightened things out. But Stephany refused and apologized for her actions. "You have every right to be upset, but I think having me here would suit your conscience. You won't be asking who I'm with and wondering all sorts of things." "You mean the sorts of things you were doing when you're supposed to be with your girlfriends? Clearly it doesn't matter if you're here or not, you're going to do what suits you. You violated our marriage in the worst way and screwed this guy in the car that I bought for you. I should castrate you." "James please with the threats, I know you're pissed, but were going to get through this." "Everyone has betrayed me, I don't want to speak with your mother because she knew all along what you were up to and didn't tell me. No worries they'll be getting a nice rent bill in the mail with the increased fees." "James please, don't, they can't afford it." "I want you out by the time I get back, you have two hours to pack what you can and get the hell out of my house." "James where are you going?" "Well I guess I can continue being honest with you although you weren't honest with me about your ware bouts. I'm headed to the BMW dealer to trade in the car and recuperate some of my money." He slammed the door and sped off down the drive way. Disgusted by the thoughts of what took place in the car, he wore gloves and put on his glasses and favored a race car driver.

The Italian dealer was disappointed that he had to return more than half of the money but tried to sell James another vehicle. When James returned home Stephany was sitting in the living room with her parents and girlfriends. All who James felt betrayed by was in attendance to regain his trust and salvage their marriage. His first thought was to conduct a massacre for their secrecy but Janet began the intervention by apologizing to James and tried to convince him that he also had their full support. But James was no push over. "So where was the intervention and support on my behalf when all of this foolishness was taking place?" Mrs. Williams confidently answered, "We were wrong for not telling you James but we all told Stephany that she was wrong and this would end badly for her but she's stubborn and made a stupid decision." Marcy jumped in with her sarcastic blunt honesty. "I told her that guy was ugly and she should have used a dildo." LOL! When the intervention was over but with no conclusion, the only person that didn't speak was Mr. Williams who was basically an observer but held a brief conversation with James when the ladies cleared the room.

Mr. Williams was able to apply empathy with James and told him how he was able to forgive his wife after discovering that she had an affair. "I'm truly sorry son and I certainly have a good understanding of what you're going through. It's obviously a case of daughter like mother. When I found out her mother had an affair I was devastated. The other guy had a grudge against me because I beat him out for the starting forward spot on the basketball team. I guess sleeping with my girl was a little pay back. Truthfully the only reason that I stayed with her mother was because I was still in love with her. I didn't pray to God or have an intervention because I knew she was still the one for me. I'm the one who decided that you and Stephany needed an intervention because I knew how you were feeling. I knew that you wanted to kill Stephany because that's what I wanted to do to her mother. Quite frankly, you still have that option but jail is no place for a man of your character. You can give Stephany a taste of her own medicine and parade with a bunch of women or get some more help and move on and have a fruitful marriage." While sipping on a corona James replied, "You know Mr. Williams some men would take this as a clear opportunity to go and explore with other women but you're right, I believe that the best option is to go and get some help and try to move forward. I actually made that decision when realizing I'm really too cute for jail but most of all, I really love Stephany and want us to have a family." Her parents were thrilled but happier that James allowed them to stay in the condo rent free. That night James remained in the guess room watching a love story on "Lifetime," where two lovers had different views on how their relationship would progress if either one of them was to marry someone else. The surprising little twist hit home for James as he remained glued to the screen. The woman said, "As long as I'm in your presence, I'll always be open to you." Her lover asked, "What about if you were married, would you still be opened to me?" She replied, "Yes I would." The woman then turned and asked him the same question and the guy said "No, not if I was married, I would not cheat on my wife with you. I wouldn't play with the both of you." The broken hearted woman conceded that was an excellent and honest answer. ok cool!

CHAPTER 6

The Therapist

JAMES AND STEPHANY both decided to seek help and attend a group counseling session along with two other couples. Steve and Carrie, was a Caucasian couple in their late twenties and were married for six years. Dave and Veronica was an African American couple in their late thirties, and were only married for two years. Everyone introduced themselves with both guys being construction workers and their wives were stay at homes mothers. Steve and Carrie had a one-month old daughter Jessica and Dave and Veronica struggled to have children. Although being emotionally drained, James was totally committed to saving his marriage but Stevie Wonder would have been distracted by the beauty of their therapist Dr. Laura Simmons. She was a stunning brunette in her early thirties who favored CNN – Out-front Anchor Erin Burnett. Dr. Simmons had recently received her PHD from Drexel University. Her sexy business suits revealed a well-toned figure and gorgeous legs. Dr. Simmons's smile was just as welcoming as her refined office. Stephany was the first to compliment her and asked "Did you do the decorations yourself? The paintings are exceptionally well done, very attractive, clean lines, inviting and sensually appealing." Dr. Simmons answered "The office was actually already staged pretty well but I wanted to apply my own personal touch." She could feel James undressing her with his eyes so she distracted him by asking the cliché question "So what brings you in today? Let's start with the Pain couple." James stated "Well I think my wife should answer that question." After taking a deep breath, Stephany nervously replied, "We're here today because I made a bad conscience decision and cheated on my husband." Ms. Simmons immediately grabbed her pad and began taking notes as to say "Oh this is going to be a good one." "Please continue Mrs. Pain." "Ok, the reason I was unfaithful in my marriage was because the sex is extremely poor. Instead of leaving my husband and finding happiness elsewhere, I was dishonest. So that's why we're here." Dr. Simmons asked "Is the sex extremely poor on your behalf or your husband's?" Steph replied "On his behalf." "Ok there's always two sides to a story. Is this true Mr. Pain.?" To some extent, but the reason why the sex has been poor on my end is because her vagina has a foul odor. I just want to get in and get out as quickly as possible." Completely shocked and humiliated Stephany jumped out of her seat and expressed her frustration, "Excuse you, that is a complete lie, and how come you never said anything the entire time? You're simply trying to justify your lackluster performance. I thought we came here to be honest with each other. I guess you pick and choose what you like to communicate."

Dr. Simmons asked, "Mr. Pain did you communicate your dis pleasure with your wife?" "No, I thought with all the feminine hygiene products that I purchased for her would have been a hint." Stephany continued, "You're a liar, I swear to God if you continue, I will get up and walk out that door and just say the hell with our marriage." Dr. Simmons was certainly amused but remained professional and got them to continue venting. Stephany continued "He's also a workaholic and rarely home, and when he is home, he's in the kitchen basically figuring out ways to boost his cholesterol and how to become a diabetic." James just sat there with no rebuttal. "What is your profession Mrs. Pain," She answered, "Before we got married I worked as a Lab Technician, I'm currently unemployed because that's what James wanted." "Ok thank you," and just to be clear, what is your profession sir?" "I'm the owner of Pain Condominiums." Dr. Simmons's world lit up. "Oh wow I saw your commercials on TV. Great slogan." (Come join the Pleasure of Pain). "Yes it's fantastic, can we get back to the issues please?" Stephany said. "Sure Mrs. Pain, let us move along to Steve and Carrie." Without hesitation Steve said, "When I took the urine test for my first construction job, I didn't know that they could tell if its female urine or male urine. I thought that they were only looking for drugs because I smoke marijuana. Anyway, the doctor walked into the office and told me, congratulations you're going to be the first guy to have a baby because you're pregnant. That's how I found out that she also cheated on me and I was arrested for a domestic dispute after beating her. I was then sentenced to these counseling sessions by the courts. I lost that job and had to settle for a temp position. Unfortunately, the father of the baby was killed in a motorcycle accident and I still love and want to be with her, it's just a really rough time for the both of us."

CORNELL RICHARDS

Carrie was speechless but started to cry. Dr. Simmons gave her a box of tissues as Veronica blurted, "Well on a lighter note, I wish I had both of your problems. I would love to have a baby, and wish my man was a workaholic and could provide for his family." James asked, I thought Dave said that he was also a construction worker?" Veronica continued Dave hasn't worked in over a year. He's at the bar from Sunday to Sunday and has a low sperm count. I am receiving food stamps and used my refund check from community college as a down payment for our apartment. That was the dumbest move I made because I should have used the money to get away from your sorry ass." Dave replied, "Well you're just as pathetic for staying with me. I would have surely taken that money, had a few drinks with my buddies and gotten the hell away from you. You dummy." "So if I'm so dumb then why are you with me Dave?" "Because you take care of everything and the sex is convenient, why the hell would I leave all those benefits on the table? So obviously I'm not that stupid." Everyone looked stunned and Dr. Simmons just shook her head before intervening. "There's obviously some trust issues here and there seems to be a lack of communication on all three sides. However, you all have taken a great step in wanting to fix your marriage. I would like to schedule everyone for Tuesdays and Thursdays starting next week. I have a strict method for success and it includes not telling your friends certain things that goes on in your marriage.

Please review the homework because during our next visit, I'll be expecting some feedback. Dr. Simmons gave them a two-page document and told them to have a nice evening. As they walked out the door, she couldn't help to notice James's muscle tight buttocks; he also caught the vibe and turned around in time to catch her smirk. When Stephany and James arrived home they began receiving phone calls. But Stephany was very short with everyone and thanked them for their support and concerns. She then took a shower and grabbed a glass of wine. James remained in the guess room watching ESPN with an explicit thought of Dr. Simmons crossing his mind. While relaxing with her glass, Stephany began reading the two-page document. It basically explained several things married couples shouldn't tell their friends. "Although it felt good to vent to friends when your spouse is driving you crazy a little complaining is fine, but once you convince friends that your significant other is a disappointment, they're not going to forget it. You may make up or get over your dispute, but your friends may not be able to do so quite easily. Here is what the Counselor recommended. "Couples already compete: Whose house is bigger? Who drives the better car? If you spill the beans about your husband's salary, friends may categorize you unfairly. You wouldn't want friends to write off your issues as unimportant because they believe you make too much money to have real problems or treat you with an air of superiority because they make more than you (although the best kinds of friends would do neither -- consciously, anyway). Maintain the balance in your friendship by keeping all financial discussions private. A friend once told me that her husband called his penis "the trunk." I had trouble looking him in the eye for months afterward. It can be thrilling to compare notes with friends about your sex lives. But there are certain details it's best to leave out -- like your partner's sexual fetishes, the size of his penis and any other tidbits you wouldn't want people to whisper about behind your back. Nearly every married couple has some debt, but how much or how little says a lot about your financial stability as a couple.

Friends may feel resentful if you brag about how little debt you and your husband have accumulated over the years. If you complain that you have too much debt, friends may not invite you to their summer house because they feel guilty that they're doing better. Don't give friends a reason to judge you. Married couples sometimes joke about whose wife or husband they'd want to sleep with. I've had friends tell me they've fantasized about another friend's husband. It's normal to have fantasies but dangerous to share them. A friend with loose lips could blow your cover -- and that could lead to all sorts of awkwardness. Don't share this one with anyone besides your hubby (and honestly, you might not even want to tell him). Don't let marriage get in the way of a good friendship. If a close friend turns your husband off (or vice versa), don't tell her or him. In fact, don't even tell your other friends -- especially if the affected pal didn't really do anything to deserve a bad rap. Don't discuss personal issues around your friend's children. They can simply mention your secrets to their parents and your home will seem more chaotic due to their exaggerations." That was actually some pretty good stuff and Steph became even more excited to get started. She then went into the guess room to give James the homework but he was fast asleep. She stood over him as he slept peacefully then rubbed his soft cheek and adjusted his pillow. It was a beautiful summer night as she gazed over the suburbs and checked her phone. There's several messages from

Roy and she's tempted to return his call but during this time Steph was able to put the Roy syndrome on cold ice.

When Steve and Carrie got home she went over the homework and he wiped her tears after another night of beating her and yelling, "You see all of this crap that you're putting me through? I lost a damn good job, went to prison because you couldn't keep your legs closed and now I have to tell my business to strangers and sit and listen to other people's garbage." She pleaded with him, "If I would have testified against you, you would have gone to jail for a really long time but remember I told the judge that you were a good man?" "Shut up bitch" and he gave her a slap across the face while she was holding the baby. "Complete animal." When Dave and Veronica reached home, Dave looked over the homework while sipping a beer and Veronica jumped on the phone, chatting away with one of her girlfriends. "I don't know why I continue to put up with this idiot?" Dave overheard and replied. "You put up with me because my sex is good," "Trust me sweetie, at best you're a four." "Hey that's good enough to keep you around, I'm consistent with my low standards, no need to overdo it." LOL! Veronica then walked over to Dave as he laid on the dingy couch and had a heart to heart with him. "Look, Dave I know things for you are a little depressing and maybe the doctors are wrong maybe it's me. But you have to meet me half way. If our marriage is going to work." "Didn't you hear the therapist say that we took a great step by attending the sessions?" He replied, "I'll fill out some applications on line but I can't make them hire me."

The next morning James took a look at the homework while having breakfast. His emotional roller coaster had begun because he didn't cook anything for Stephany. When she awoke expecting a meal, he blurted "Since I'm so busy figuring out how to raise my cholesterol and become a diabetic, I didn't want to endanger you. So until I learn how to cook more nutritiously, we can prepare our food separately." "You're being an asshole," "That's what you told the therapist; these are your words, not mine, so you're the asshole." She poured herself a glass of orange juice as he continued. "That's the problem with you black women, you want to play games, cheat and manipulate and still receive all the benefits in your relationship." She hurled the glass of orange juice across the room and it landed directly in his breakfast. She then shouted, then why don't you get a white woman since you think they're any better and all will be well, you're not going to hold me hostage for what I did. I'm accepting responsibility and willing to work it out." "Yeah that's easy for you to say since you've done so much damage." He cleaned off the table and threw away his caramel waffles topped with whip cream and strawberries. Fixing their marriage was a high priority but Stephany wanted to live an all-around healthier lifestyle. After she made a few suggestions that were ignored for them to join a gym, Steph finally signed up and received her membership from Lucille Roberts. It was actually the looks of Dr. Simmons that ignited Steph to sign up. She knew that James thought the doctor was hot and felt intimidated but clearly was in no position to question his thoughts about their gorgeous new therapist. It was now time for their first session. They were scheduled for 4pm that Tuesday but James arrived a half hour early. He sat patiently outside of Dr. Simmons office hoping to spend some extra time with her. The two other couples had also arrived. It was raining that day and Stephany showed up with her hair looking crazy. She complained about a cab splashing a puddle of water on her. Dr. Simmons entered the waiting room looking radiant and acknowledged them both while escorting her previous clients out the door.

Stephany went to the lady's room and tried her best to get herself together; but it was one of those days that no matter how hard she tried to make it better, it was just meant for her to have a bad day. Dr. Simmons returned and she proudly welcomed them back. "Well hello again, despite the rain which I see has caused some discomfort, I'm happy everyone was able to make it back. So let's get straight to business. What do you both think about your first homework assignment?" Stephany mentioned, I thought the tips were very helpful, but I'll honestly struggle with it a little because I share a lot with my girlfriends, especially my older friend Janet." That statement irritated James. "So you're confiding in your friends instead of the man you married, and obviously your friends are not the only ones you've been sharing with. Excellent job Steph." "Mr. Pain please allow her to continue and don't interrupt again." Dr. Simmons's austerity was a complete turn on. Stephany continued and asked, "Well during this process, who's supposed to be my support system if James is pissing me off, how about my parents? I have a wonderful relationship with my mother, and I was working on the relationship between my mother in- law but I don't know how that's going to work out now." Dr. Simmons answered her questions. "Mrs. Pain having a support system is tremendous and extremely vital, however James is correct, no matter what issues you're having you're always supposed to run towards your partner not to your girlfriends, even if you think its great advice, because their great advice could be cancerous for your relationship. And that also goes for the men. Mr. Pain I'm not sure if you have any male friends that you often vent with but, I highly recommend that after an argument there should be no texting your friends and parents making them aware of your dispute." James replied, "You might as well have just told her to go and move a mountain. She is totally incapable of doing that."

Stephany just looked at him and folded her arms and agreed that she should have kept her issues within the household. During the second session, everyone was once again on time. But James appeared to now being a little doubtful and cavalier. Dr. Simmons became annoyed with James not doing the work and studying the material. She then asked would he like to see a psychiatrist which they would prescribe medication for his mood swings. He declined and offered a heart melting elaboration of the kind of woman he needs in his life. "I don't need to see a psychiatrist or to be medicated. However, what I am in desperate need for is a woman that is loyal and has enough respect for me to communicate and not behave like a whore. Ok, I haven't been reading the material, instead I've been secretly reading this book called Creating A Housewife. It's about this guy intentionally seeking a whore to turn her into a respectable housewife, awesome book and maybe I should introduce Stephany to him. LOL! If you can think of the greatest love songs in history, that's how I treat this woman ten times over and I need someone who appreciates that by simply saying "thank you" and maybe a massage once in a while. You think Tyrese, Al Green, or Trey Songz and all those guys making hit records for women never had a bad day in the bedroom?" Stephany fired back, "We're not talking about once or twice James this was happening even before we were married." James then pulled out his new iPhone and shows the group and Dr. Simmons pictures of their beautiful home and the i8. Everyone was impressed but the guys were disappointed when James mentioned that he returned the car back to the dealer after the affair. They wanted to feel the thrill of being behind a car with such power. Overall Veronica and Carrie thought Stephany was a complete fool and Dr. Simmons was fascinated by James.

He spoke with conviction and gained her sympathy by spewing his pain. Stephany asked "How are we going to ever get passed this if you keep talking about it?" Dr. Simmons answered "Well that's the point of us being here Mrs. Pain for us to communicate and find a resolution, but first we must have a clear understanding of each other's feelings. Please James continue." "I don't speak to her at all when we're home because that's my only piece of mind and I don't want to taint my home. God only knows if this other man knows the colors of my bedroom. Ok here is some truth Dr. Simmons. I did lie about Stephany having a bad odor in her vagina. I only said that so she could feel just a fraction of the embarrassment that she caused me. The problem I'm having with her is, she thinks everything is supposed to run smooth and instantly return back to normal. Now that I think about it, I honestly might be a sucker for love. She really didn't do anything to deserve all the pleasures that I've provided for her. She's frustrated because she has to now work in order to retrieve those luxuries." Dr. Simmons took a sip of water giving herself a break from James venting. She's falling hard for him but did a great job creating equal grounds by not allowing either party to be interrupted. It was Stephany now who was having doubts that their marriage could be saved. She had now become severely sexually frustrated becomes James wasn't making any attempts to please her. He was completely turned off and emotionally distraught. Thoughts of the numerous positions that Stephany adjusted herself in to satisfy Roy were stifling. Roy eventually moved on and now has his boss in those same positions and was recently promoted to night shift supervisor. LOL! Stephany's mother sent a text to find out how things were going and she lied and said that, "All is well and we're making a lot of progress. The therapist has been very helpful and glad we both decided to go. James and I will be just fine." James checked his phone and saw Mrs. Williams message and Stephany's constant lies and thought to himself. "If this chick is lying to her mother about our progress, then how can I believe anything she's saying to me is true?" He thought about telling her the truth about hacking her cellphone. But the only person that needed to hear the truth was Dr. Simmons. He needed the right time to let her know how he's been feeling since their initial contact.

CHAPTER 7

Brutal

JAMES REALLY WASN'T a social butterfly but a little male bonding would benefit the process. So he invited Steve and Dave over to his man cave for a guy's night. "Man this is one sick house," Steve raved. Dave couldn't wait to get his hands on a cold one and stated, "Ok let's talk about the pink elephant in the room. Dr. Simmons is so gorgeous," James was modest, "Yeah she's not bad looking." Dave replied, "Come on bro, you had to notice her checking you out. Especially when you flashed those photos of the car. Hell my eyes lit up. LOL! You should go for it, the worst thing that could happened is she saying no." "Hey I'm with you either way, I don't know many guys that slept with their therapist. And a little pay back wouldn't hurt." Steve said. "Well I guess it depends if you really want to stay in your marriage or not?" Dave asked. James answered, "You know sometimes I have my days where I could care less and then there are days when I still want to be a family." The guys were in agreeance with him and then respectively asked for a job recommendation. James replied that the construction company that does work on his building has a great union and he would be sure to mention both of them for the clean-up crew. Steve then shared pictures of baby Jessica with the guys congratulating him for stepping up to the plate but James admitted, "Now if Steph would have gotten pregnant I would have signed those divorced papers in a hurry. You're certainly a better man then me Steve."

A few weeks later James decided to switch lanes by taking the focus off saving his marriage and sought treatment to save himself from ruining future relationships because of his sex issues. He felt comfortable with Dr. Simmons and she already gained his trust. So he secretly scheduled one-on-one meetings to see the therapist but kept the guys updated. It was certainly unethical accepting James as a client behind his wife's back while still having them both as clients and not terminating their sessions. But Ms. Simmons was a young doctor and had bills to pay which James doubled her fees and paid them in advance. He would see her once a week which brought the total visits to three times. During his visits with Dr. Simmons there would be quite a bit of flirting which turned into serious probing. "James are you having a problem physically or emotionally causing you to have bad sex? I don't have a problem getting an erection, I guess it would be emotionally. It feels terrible to have a nice size penis but don't have a clue on how to use it." His candor caused her to smirk while taking notes. "James just to help me make a better assessment, "How many women have you slept with in your entire life." That certainly caught him by surprise but he answered, "I've been with twelve women including my wife." "Ok and how many times did you have this issue?" "I had this issue with half of them." "Interesting, you've only been with a dozen women but yet you've only had negative experiences with half of them. So how did the relationship end with the ones that you had good experiences with?" "Well truthfully either I was good or they didn't want to hurt my feelings and just flaked out because I was working hard in college and then always competed for that top promotion, which led me to now becoming an owner."

"James, please allow me to confuse you. You have an issue but you don't have an issue, which causes an issue. He looked confused. You're not working to over compensate a void in your life which so many people often do, you just haven't attacked this issue as much as you would do with your career. So when it's time to become intimate that's when you have an issue along with the strong possibilities of bad chemistry that may have occurred with the women that you chose to sleep with including your wife." "Wow that was powerful, I see someone paid attention in school." She revealed her beautiful smile while asking in a soft and sexy tone, "Do you feel like you're getting your monies worth?" He replied "Absolutely" James was instructed to keep his personal life private but he informed the therapist that he wanted to ask his Facebook family a very interesting question that could help him emotionally. "Soo much emphasis is placed on sex I sure hope some people can be honest or they might feel too ashamed to answer such a thought provoking personal question on social media." LOL. The therapist agreed, "Yes James this is a very sensitive topic and you'll be surprised about the number of people who are secretly experiencing these issues but can't afford the resources to get help. I'll keep an eye out for your post tonight and see how this works out for you. Today was a great day and we accomplished a lot. I'll see you and Stephany tomorrow."

Later that evening he went home and didn't cook anything. Although filled with eager he doesn't expose details of his failing marriage and posted, "Ladies If you met a guy that was the best guy in the world and he treated you like the Queen you are but his sex performance was absolutely garbage would you A. Stay and get some good loving on the side? B. Stay and make it work? or C. Leave and find happiness elsewhere? After receiving some well anticipated mixed answers, most replies were in favor of "Staying and making it work," and explained. "After a while sex fades away no matter how much you try to keep the fire burning, it's ultimately the good love that allows the relationship to thrive? He thanked everyone for their comments with a few poking fun at the question by asking, "Was he having trouble in paradise?" He replied that all was well and that he saw the question in a magazine article and just wanted to share. The next day Stephany complained about not feeling well and insisted that James should go without her. He mumbled under his breath, "I don't give a damn if you go or not. You can stay here and chit chat with your ugly ass boyfriend." When he arrived at the office Dr. Simmons was all smiles. "Well hello, great post, how are you feeling?" "I'm terrific, but unfortunately my wife claimed to not be feeling well, so you're stuck with just me again. But I won't keep you for the entire time because others may be more in need of your services and might not be in good spirits such as myself." His thoughtfulness and concern for others was orgasmic. That evening the tables had turned and James gave her the floor and learned just how much Dr. Simmons loved to talk about herself. She was also from South Philly but of course had never met Stephany. Her parents were retired police officers but were divorced. She loved babies but had none of her own and thought the world of her niece and nephew which her older brother had been married for ten years. The conversation turned extra casual when Dr. Simmons mentioned that she was single and recently experienced a bad relationship which resulted in her having to get a restraining order against her previous boyfriend. By the time she finished talking his head off, they were well over the original scheduled time. She apologized to her other clients and said goodbye to James.

Stephany missed three straight meetings which led to Dr. Simmons canceling her sessions entirely.

New Town Square is getting pounded with heavy thunderstorms and James had become a prisoner in his own home. The gorgeous guess room was basically solitary confinement. After making a delicious grill cheese sandwich with tomato soup for lunch, he returned back to his comfort zone. The safety of his immaculate home was a main concern so he went back on his word and left Stephany's food in the microwave. He was the best at arranging business meetings but was now struggling to position himself in a setting that would not be awkward between him and the therapist. Regardless of the vibes she has been giving him, several sessions had passed and she could have come to her senses and changed her mind. But of course being a good business man meant that you have to take chances. So he simply picked up the phone and called late in the afternoon. Luckily for him she was preparing to take her lunch break but was glad to hear his voice after her assistant transferred his call. He lied about already being on the road and asked could he stop by her office. "I would like to bring something to your attention Dr. Simmons but I don't want to talk and drive at the same time because the weather is bad." Filled with suspense of what could be on his mind, she replied, "Sure Mr. Pain I'll let my secretary Monica know that I'm expecting you." He threw on some sweatpants and a T-shirt as Steph remained in bed taking a nap. When James arrived his T-shirt was soaked and glued to his chiseled chess and huge biceps. He was the highlight of the secretary's day as she confirmed his arrival and said, "Wooo girl whatever is wrong with this one, please let me fix him, Sheeessh." Seconds later, Dr. Simmons welcomed James into her office. Amazing, right before they began chatting, the storm ended, followed by a rainbow and a bright sunshine.

The clouds eventually returned but the evening was filled with laughs and a decent level of comfort. Dr. Simmons opened herself up like a 24-hour convenient store. "Oh Please, call me Laura" "Ok, that name really fits your persona." "Thank you. I've been a therapist for two years now and I would say that the two most stressful professionals are lawyers and medical doctors. Teachers would be third or perhaps not in that exact order." He admired her humbleness by not selecting her profession as the most stressful because of having to listen to all of the others. She then added, "But I guess receiving some free tickets to the Eagles first two home games as a bonus isn't bad. I got them from a lawyer who is a season ticket holder. It's really tough rooting for the Eagles but being born in South Philly you're pretty much baptized at birth as a fan." LOL! When I was a little girl my parents couldn't afford to go to the games so they always made sure we went to their practices. I remember cheering for Randall Cunningham and that great 90's Eagles team." After seeing her gym membership on her desk for Lucille Roberts. He said, "A woman at the gym is sexier than a woman at the club." "Why thank you James." He then asked, "So what do you enjoy doing in your spare time when granted?" "That sure is rare, well the usual stuff, a good movie and dinner date would be nice or a theater play. I love ice skating and traveling but haven't had much time to do either." For a quick second Dr. Simmons accelerated her aggression. "James you're very attractive and you have juicy lips." "Thank you for the compliment." "It wasn't a compliment, it's a mandatory characteristic." She then snapped back to reality, "Wait a minute, I'm saying way too much, this sounds like an interview for a relationship. What am I doing? You're married." James was clever, "At least I'm providing a sympathetic ear and not judging you. We're just two adults having a regular conversation. Sometimes that's all that's needed to bring joy and peace to someone's heart. How do you feel?" "I don't know how I feel; I'm having trouble explaining it. But it sure feels good. No this is wrong." At this point there was certainly nothing to lose, so he confessed. "For the past month you've been weighing heavy on my conscience. I just need you to tell me that I'm wrong and that you don't feel the same." There's a brief silence but she remained professional by replying with a text book answer, "Excuse me Mr. Pain, I am your therapist and my job is to help you resolve your issues in your rela... Before she could finish he lunged himself at her which she held him with more intensity while kissing. She had no clue what kind of cologne he was wearing but he smelled so good. She paused, then poked her head outside of the door to send her secretary on a lunch run. She then kicked off her heels while James shoved his hands up her skirt and removed her panties. She was about to remove her glasses but James told her to keep them on. He was turned on by the sophistication. He's at full attention as she removed the gold wrapper from a magnum latex, then grabbed hold of his electrifying cord and plugged it into her yearning socket. They started off great but minutes later James had a short circuit. Dr. Simmons reaction could not have been any colder. "Ok, now I see what your wife was talking about. That was downright awful. I never thought I would live to see someone screw up a quickie." LOL! "I can't believe I put my entire career on the line for that." Actually it was perfect timing because the secretary knocked on the door with her lunch order. While getting dressed his face was filled with total humiliation and regret, but she was confident that he was a working progress and could be fixed. So James got a pass. "Hey, I want to see you again" She assured him that everything was going to be alright. She actually thought James's over excitement was cute in a weird sort of way. Dr. Simmons then asked him to accompany her at the Eagles home opener against the Redskins for the 2014 season. He accepted. But he just sadly nodded his head and said "ok" then left her office. He seemed totally incompetent and it was only her second year as a licensed therapist but Dr. Laura Simmons was the best in the city. She also had high referrals and recommendations from more established Doctors but was destined to do things her way. Establishing common ground, mixed with a little fun would be her strategy for a fresh start and to reassure comfort. James came to her with his confidence shot and her words could have driven a weaker man to become suicidal.

James needed his support system FAST, so he called the guys and met up with them at a tavern in the city. Frustrated with himself, James held his head down while sitting at the bar and explained how he blew it with Dr. Simmons. "Man things were flowing, she was wearing this crazy matching black and pink Victoria Secret bra and panties and after she strapped me up, I must have came after three strokes." Steve couldn't help but to burst out laughing but tried to cheer him up and said, "If you were able to accomplish something that was damn near impossible, who's going to complain that you did a bad job achieving the goal. That's like saying you won the NBA Championship but only scored three points the entire game. Who the hell cares, man you nailed your therapist." Dave was more sympathetic to James's feelings. "Man, I see where you're coming from. You really wanted to impress her, maybe you were just nervous. Was the light shining bright in the office?" "No, not really" "Oh well it's hard for me to concentrate with the light in my eye. I need the room to be dim." "Steve said, man I don't care if its broad day light, I'm going to handle my business and hers." Dave added, "But wait you said that she wants to see you again and take you to an Eagles game, well you couldn't have done that bad of a job. Just go and see what happens, hey at least you'll be having the pleasure of business. LOL! But I still say go to the game, you'll be more relaxed for the next time around." James agreed with both men and was back in good spirits after the third round of beers.

CHAPTER 8

Game Time

I T'S A ONE o'clock kick off to start the Eagle's 2014 season. Dr. Simmons was looking like a true fan with her eye black painting, Eagle's Jersey and ripped jeans as James wore the same and they were seated at mid field. She was excited and full of smiles every time the Eagles made a great play. Dr. Simmons's plan seemed to be working perfectly to get him to be more relaxed and to be himself. Her evaluation of James's issues were based on the fact that the constant need to impress had taken a toll on him in the bedroom. James was experiencing anxiety attacks when his adrenaline rushed causing him to have premature ejaculation. By allowing him to express his frustration on every bad play that the Eagles made loosened him up. She remembered that some of her colleagues usually recommended visiting a gun rage or hitting a punching bag to release tension. Those options would be suggested if James didn't do well for the first test. The supportive home crowd cheered their team all the way to victory and James admitted he felt different and more confident in himself. "I actually feel less stressed and like some weight was removed from my shoulders." That's all the Doctor needed to hear. It wouldn't be wise to go back to the office because it would have given him flashbacks and made him nervous. So she took a chance and they went back to her place. It's truly something special when a person "Has their mind right." They're chemistry had clicked, and upon opening the door of her beautifully furnished bachelorette pad. James snatched off her jersey as she laid on the bed looking like a sexy cheerleader in her black bra and face still painted. She blessed him orally then after he exploded in her mouth. The only issue now was to get him to take a break.

"Oh my god that was amazing," she said while lying on his chest. After round five she was exhausted, "I think I created a monster. Come on pretty boy your wife is going to be expecting you home soon, the game was over three hours ago." "Actually the game is just starting, seems like I'm not the only one that needs to be relaxed." "You're funny, very charming and a girl could get use to this sort of treatment." "Your back is so tensed. He gave her a nice massage before putting on his clothes and leaving. The next time the guys met up with James, they were back at his place giving him hi fives. Dave asked, "See aren't you glad you accepted her offer? She's basically upgrading you." James replied, "I'm really learning that sex is a psychological aspect. I have so much confidence in myself now. It's like she verbally gave me a brain sex pill." Steve then asked a dumb question. "So are you going to see her again?" "Absolutely," James replied. Steve continued, "I thought this was just a one-time thing. Don't you think that your ongoing relationship might interfere with the counseling process?" James answered "Hmmm... "Not at all because I respect her authority. We've all heard of the bad case of mixing business with pleasure going horribly wrong but the level of respect that I have for Dr. Simmons goes beyond our relationship in the bedroom." "But how long could you keep up the charade?" Steve asked. Dave specified, "The question is what's the purpose?" "I'm not really sure if I want to be with my wife anymore and Dr. Simmons has given me new life. Since I can't afford to have drama on both sides of the board then divorcing Stephany would be the best option. But a woman's intuition is the most vital sense that she was blessed with and it begins to pound on Stephany's conscience. He hasn't given her any feedback from the sessions and hasn't even attempted to sleep with her. So one day she invaded the man cave as he was relaxing. She snatched off his headphones and began nagging him. "Ok, so I understand that you're still hurting but how about a little more communication James. What's going on at therapy?" "Nothing much, just a bunch of stuff Dr. Simmons is blabbering about that people with common sense don't apply." "No James, something else is going on, she had to say more than that." "Ok what's going on is that, we probably don't have great chemistry together and that's why I'm turned off by you." "Really, are you trying to be funny? That's a load of crap, is that what she said?" "Look the most important thing is that I'm still going, sorry you were sick and got kicked out." Stephany threw the headphones on the couch and stomped up the stairs.

The very next day she stormed into Dr. Simmons's office. Luckily there were no clients there but Monica the secretary threatened to call the police. Horrified that Stephany found out about the affair but remaining calm Dr. Simmons said, "It's ok Monica, Mrs. Pain please sit down. Well I'm certainly glad to see that you're feeling better, would you like to rejoin the group?" "Hell no, you've been feeding my husband a bunch of garbage." Dr. Simmons thought to herself, "Well actually he loves the taste of what I've been feeding him." LOL! "But replied I don't understand." Stephany became irritated and flew off the couch, their now face to face and she asked, "Did you tell my husband that there was no chemistry between us and that I turn him off?" Dr. Simmons apologized for the confusion and admitted to having a poor choice of words. "That was a complete error on my behalf." With that response, the wild beast is calmed but Stephany gave an unexpected response of her own as they remained face to face, "Damn you're gorgeous." "Thank you Mrs. Pain" while slowly backing away. Dr. Simmons continued to sympathize and apply empathy. "This is certainly a rough and confusing time for you. However, although you are not a part of the group, I'm still here to help you. James has been participating well. How are things at home? Better I assume." "James has been acting like a jerk, he hasn't touched me, he no longer cooks for me out of love, he only cooks out of fear that I'll mistakenly burn the house down. I should be the one apologizing to you, I guess if it wasn't for you, James and I would be nonexistent." What a funny twist, James's infidelity is saving their marriage. Stephany continued to praise the traitor. "This might be a little overboard but would you like to have dinner with our family? It makes sense to have you over for a meal since you've already seen our dirty laundry." With that statement Dr. Simmons recalled James having very nice clean underwear that hugged his thrilling package before accepting and saying, "That sounds like a wonderful idea. Thank you."

It's actually a terrible idea and when Stephany left the office, Dr. Simmons tells her secretary to "Get James on the phone. That woman is out of her mind." He answered on the first ring and Dr. Simmons told him everything that happened but he thought she was joking. "No way, you're kidding. So why the hell didn't you just say no in a nice professional way?" "Because she was furious James, we almost came to blows, and why haven't you been having sex with her?" "I just haven't been in the mood" Dr. Simmons replied, "You know what, I think you're just saving all the goods for me." "Maybe, maybe not? But come to think of it, this isn't going to be so bad, I get to cook for you and I'll have both of my women in the same room." "Ha ha ha, you're so bad, but it won't be the setting you're expecting because she's also inviting your parents so you'll have to behave." "Ok cool. So when is this craziness supposed to take place?" "I guess you'll have to let me know, she didn't say, I'm hoping she changes her mind," "Or maybe she'll just forget about the whole thing." Seconds later Stephany came in the room and said "I invited the therapist and our parents for dinner, can you call Dr. Simmons and ask is Friday night at eight ok?" He disappointedly shook his head, then whispered, "Is Friday night at eight ok? Hahaha! "Yeah that's fine, I'll be there." "You can't miss us it's the best house on the block." James then called the guys on a three-way line and filled them in on the foolery. Steve thought "Man this is getting way of control, I guess it would have been better if Stephany would have hit Dr. Simmons and gone to jail, and then you ran off with the therapist." LOL! Dave agreed, "Yes this is beyond madness but let's see how it plays out." Friday night arrived in a flash and their parents were delighted to meet Dr. Simmons and honored to be a part of the helping process. James prepared a luscious butter sauce tilapia with string beans and brown rice. Dr. Simmons offered some great compliments for their spectacular home and brought along two bottles of wine that went perfect with the meal. Right before everyone was seated, Dr. Simmons asked Stephany's parents to sit next to James and James's parents to sit next to Stephany. She then explained her reason for the unusual seating arrangement. "I didn't want the feeling of A vs B team, I wanted to remove the couple from their parents wing and make them feel awkward. It's important for both James and Stephany to know that both sides of parents will show equal support." She then kept the parents on a pedestal "This couple is so blessed to have such a wonderful support system, such a beautiful family." Mrs. Williams then uttered "It would be nice if their marriage would continue and have a great addition, we've longed for grandchildren and we're totally embarrassed that this trouble has fallen upon our Stephany." James's father replied "Excuse me but I think your Stephany is the one to blame for the trouble that has been caused. Remember she cheated on our son with that scare crow."

Mr. Williams tried to defend his wife but knew all too well the pain James was feeling. Dr. Simmons explained "This is actually great for the healing process because everyone is getting their anger out and saying how they really feel. So we can eventually move on. We've all made some bad choices but what's most important is that this couple remains strong and the only way that will happen is if everyone remains unified." Everyone looked around at each other and agreed. After dinner, James offered an unusual desert that was meant for breakfast but since he had everyone around that was important to him in the room, he took a chance and was anxious to hear their opinions. His simple recipe of putting apple sauce on a raisin bagel was delicious. He explained, "I was just bored one day and ran out of jelly so I tried something new. What do you guy's think?" Everyone asked for seconds but he ran out of bagels so they took an extra plate of food instead. It was a perfect evening, Steph and James thanked them for coming and he walked everyone back to their cars. When James returned Steph was laced in all-black lingerie. Completely fed up with his avoidance, she tried to force herself on him and yelled, "It's been months since we last made love. "Ok not a problem" he thought, and he gave her three minutes of hell. Surprisingly she's satisfied. It's been that long that Stephany now appreciates bad sex. So Sad! Her good friend Janet decides to send her a text message just to check in to see how she was doing and mentioned "Trust me girl there are some women out here that really have some issues, just take a look at what popped up in my spam mail today, I just shared it on Facebook and it already has over a three hundred Likes."

"Dear Husband:

I'm writing you this letter to tell you that I'm leaving you for good. I've been a good woman to you for seven years and I have nothing to show for it. These last two weeks have been hell. Your boss called to tell me that you had quit your job today and that was the last straw.

Last week, you came home and didn't notice that I had gotten my hair and nails done, cooked your favorite meal and even wore a brand new negligee. You came home and ate in two minutes, and went straight to sleep after watching the game. You don't tell me you love me anymore; you don't touch me or anything. Either you're cheating or you don't love me anymore, whatever the case is. I'm gone.

P.S. If you're trying to find me, don't. Your BROTHER and I are moving away to West Virginia together. Have a great life. Surprisingly the husband replied,

"Dear Ex-Wife:

Nothing has made my day more than receiving your letter. It's true that you and I have been married for seven years, although a good woman is a far cry from what you've been. I watch sports so much to try to drown out your constant nagging. Too bad that doesn't work.

I did notice when you cut off all of your hair last week, the first thing that came to mind was "You look just like a man!" My mother raised me to not say anything if you can't say anything nice. When you cooked my favorite meal, you must have gotten me confused with MY BROTHER, because I stopped eating pork seven years ago. I went to sleep on you when you had on that new negligee because the price tag was still on it. I prayed that it was a coincidence that my brother had just borrowed fifty dollars from me that morning and your negligee was $49.99. After all of this, I still loved you and felt that we could work it out. So when I discovered that I had hit the lotto for ten million dollars, I quit my job and bought us two tickets to Jamaica. But when I got home you were gone. Everything happens for a reason I guess. I hope you have the fulfilling life you always wanted. My lawyer said with your letter that you wrote, you won't get a dime from me. So take care.

P.S. I don't know if I ever told you this but Carl, my brother was born Carla. I hope that's not a problem." "That was hilarious." Stephany replied. Both women then planned a lady's night out before Steph mentioned that her counseling sessions were a complete waste of time.

CHAPTER 9

New Job

I T WAS A Friday morning when Janet called to confirm a location for their evening out. Steph said "Just somewhere to relax and have some fun, I really need a few laughs. I haven't done so in months." "Ok, well of course Marcy's silly behind could help you with that and I know she probably has a few places in mind." James didn't plan on doing much, in fact he was happy to hear that she was going out with her girlfriends so he could have the house to himself to chillax. Stephany didn't say exactly where they were going and James was now feeling the effects of sexual exhaustion from his week-long encounters with Dr. Simmons. Later that evening Stephany's dark blue jeans look like she painted them on her body and sporting a red top and matching heels. She met with the girls in the city and they're all excited about being reunited. Marcy couldn't wait to start, "So how was rehab?" "It sure felt like rehab. Where are we going?" The summer had ended but it was a beautiful night as Marcy explained, "We're going to see this special guest at this function tonight, it's a fun event. They'll have food and drinks and afterwards live entertainment. I heard about this guy from a few folks at work who calls himself the whipper. He guarantees that after implementing his good love strategies your man will be whipped and won't be able to keep his hands off you. They said he's also pretty funny so let's see." There was a full house and diverse atmosphere of all ages in attendance to see, "The Whipper." The trio had ordered their drinks, laughed and just got reacquainted with each other. The hostess, who was a young beautiful casually dressed Caucasian girl finally announced the man of the hour and all were ecstatic with his philosophy on how men need to specialize in keeping the fire in their relationship since it was men who statistics say are more prone to cheat. "Men should try and give their woman oral sex while she's driving a car, be more attentive with the kids while she watches sports or a movie." He received a round of applause.

Back home, James decided to have company and the fellas came over for a few rounds of pool. But they eventually got bored. Dave suggested that they hit the town and glance at some eye candy. James was re-energized and thought it would be a pretty good idea. Dave then mentioned "Hey I've been hearing a lot about this guy who calls himself The Whipper. He guarantees that after you apply his techniques, your girl won't be able to keep her hands off you. Well you don't count James, you're now getting all that you can handle." Steve was on board, "Yeah I heard of that guy, I've never seen him but heard that he has some pretty good stuff. Hey, no shame in my game, anything to make that department better, I'm all ears." So James quickly changed and they also went to see the whipper." When the guys walked in, "The Whipper" was still on stage and the crowed went into an uproar when he mentioned. "You know, some guys still don't get it, "A woman only turns into a nut and starts being erratic if the sex is good. I had two bad relationships and they both ended with drama. If a guy isn't sexing his girl right, he will have less drama when it's time to break up. If the sex is great between you and your girl, then when it's time to break up, bets believe there's going to be some drama. If the woman doesn't put up a fight for you, then either because she already has some good dick on the side or she doesn't love you anymore." Woowww, the crowd erupted with Stephany and her girlfriends cheering and giving the highest praise. Stephany and James then made eye contact with Steve asking, "Hey isn't that your wife over there cheering for that guy?" James just stood there completely mortified. To add insult to injury the hostess then told everyone to "Please give another round of applause for Roy, aka "The Whipper." LOL.

What a damn shame. Now of course James is in no position to point the finger, he's been running through Dr. Simmons like a hot knife cutting butter. James then gave her girlfriends a pathetic look which was appropriate for their assistants. He attempted to walk over and drag Stephany outside but the guys grabbed him and they made a quick exit. There was complete silence in the car but James was just trying to figure out his next move or was this the last straw? It was still very early, but Steve decided to call it a night and James gave him a ride home. Maybe James's despair made him more appreciative towards his own wife. James and Dave then decided to stop by a local chain restaurant. The bar tender who was a slim, older looking blonde, with dark mascara had a look on her face that coldly read, "You black bastards better be lucky this isn't 1834." The bar tender even began straightening her ponytail before handing them menus. Dave was highly concerned about eggs or Mayonnaises being in the pasta sauce so James suggested a light butter sauce. Dave could see that although his friend was hurting, he was still concerned about his food allergies. Just as a distraction from the psychological pain Dave told a quick funny story about a pass failed relationship with an ex-girlfriend. "Wow man, I've never been lucky enough to have that kind of drama. A few years ago I saw this woman who I was very interested in but she was married at the time. When we reacquainted on social media, she told me her seven-year marriage had recently ended. Now, usually the first few dates are the beginning of the fire stage but instead things between us began getting pretty bumpy. She was thirty-eight and had no children but would often say that family meant the world to her. Oddly her future plans were to purchase a duplex and live above the tenants who would be complete strangers. But when she finally made enough money she was going to purchase a house so big, that she wouldn't be able to see her own family when they came visit. She was quite anal and I believe she had lice in her hair. She also worked as a branch manager for a bank located in the suburbs and boasted about having great communication but stood me up three times. I was a glutton for punishment. When her birthday arrived that January, I went to her job to surprise her with two balloons and some cupcakes. She had off that day and was in New York. But when I finally spoke to her I mentioned the gifts were at my home waiting for her and she never came and picked them up. I bet if I said there was 3,200 dollars waiting for her, she would have flown to my house. Oh and this bitch lives approximately three blocks away from my home. Terrible!

The last time she stood me up, she texted several hours later and asked, was I mad at her? I never replied because I was simply turned off by such juvenile behavior." She sent another text asking the same question. I never replied. She finally ended by sending another text message wishing me happy 33rd birthday and great blessings in life. I never replied. It was unbelievable, borderline insanity and pure selfishness. I thought to myself after all of her texting, why couldn't she just send a text message in the first place saying she couldn't make it instead of having me wait around like an idiot. She later in boxed me on Facebook insulting me for not having a car and still walking. I then viewed her entire profile and replied, by the looks of your pictures you should try and do a little walking yourself, as she began gaining a massive amount of weight." Dave was able to get a smile and light chuckle out of James after telling the small tale. James replied, "Yeah man that's pretty pathetic, with all the ways to communicate nowadays that's just totally unnecessary. Women like that deserve to end up with trash because that's how they conduct themselves. However they act, that's what they attract." "It was very disappointing because she had so much potential," James disagreed, "No she didn't, those were the early red flags showing you that she wasn't the one for you. So she can be someone else's headache. That is blatantly disrespectful and inconsiderate. And it was still in the beginning of the relationship so imagine how she's going to act when she really got comfortable." "All true, a woman at that age, with that profession, who either doesn't know or completely disregards the fundamentals of a relationship clearly isn't worth my time. But I hope she's doing well." The story helped along with a double shot of patron that went down quite smoothly. Overall the service was great so the bar tender received a generous tip. But the reality of the pending clash between James and Stephany awaited. Dave coached, "Look it's a confusing time right now but all you have to do is ask whether or not she's still sleeping with this guy? If she is, then you can either keep trying to fix the marriage or go your separate ways because from the looks of things, neither of you is to be trusted. But just play it cool, right now she's probably expecting the clash of the titans to take place when you arrive home. Because of everything that's been going on between you and Simmons, your hands are basically tide." James gave a slight nod in agreeance before dropping him off and heading home. On the other hand, the ladies were dumbfounded and offered no words of encouragement when giving Stephany a ride home. But Marcy did apologize and said that they had no clue that the surprise guest would be Roy. Janet offered her apology that was basically ignored and Stephany regretted not listening to Dr. Simmons by not allowing your girlfriends advice and behavior to influence your relationship. Instead of going out with their friends when feeling bored, Stephany and James should have gone out with each other. James reached home first, took a shower and returned to the guest room with his headphones blasting Drake's sophomore album "Take Care." It's a little after midnight and he couldn't hear when she opened the front door, it's her strong fragrance he smelled that caused him to remove the headphones and prepare for the confrontation. He's still a bit intoxicated but remembered what Dave said about playing it cool because of his ongoing affair with Dr. Simmons.

She immediately apologized after closing the door behind her and he remained at the top of the stairs. "I had no clue that Roy would be there tonight, it was supposed to be just us girls." "Doesn't matter, once you saw that it was him you should have left" "Ok, so what if you saw me leaving, wouldn't that have made me look suspiciously guilty?" She had a good point but he replied, "Well I guess that would have been better than standing with my friends watching you clap for another guy that's screwing you better than me. Seems like whenever you're around those two witches that's when all of the trouble starts. We were doing so well, ok another setback, but I need to know are you still sleeping with him?" "Absolutely not, we have not communicated at all." That was the truth because James also checked her email and text messages once he got home. This was an accident, but he purposely made plans for Dr. Simmons to sit on his face during his next visit. The next visit was at her apartment where she consoled him after he told her everything that happend. To help ease the stress she suggested "You're always cooking for people James, relax and put your feet up. Let me make you something to eat." She then popped a Healthy Choice dinner in the microwave. LOL! It was actually pretty good. After massaging his back, they had a heart to heart and she confessed to have fallen in love with him. "The other day I accidentally called one of my clients your name. I also mistakenly wrote your name on a new client document and I'm willing to wait until things get squared away with you and Stephany. I usually don't wait for anyone so this is totally uncharacteristic of me but that's when it was clear of how I was feeling about you. He was shocked, especially about her willing to wait. Dr. Simmons was worth it, and if he was going to leave Stephany it would make plenty of sense that she would be a better fit. He loved being a married man and loved what Dr. Simmons brought to the table. It wasn't about the sex; Dr. Simmons was just an all-around better person than Stephany.

But Dr. Simmons realized how hard she had fallen and prepared herself for the worst. So to help her cope, she decided to see a therapist. What an interesting turn of events. She hired an older white male by the name of Dr. Clark. Clark had been a therapist for twenty-five years and was brutally honest when Dr. Simmons revealed her transgressions. They visited once a week in his traditional style office that was also located in the city. She confessed, "I totally lost control, this is certainly rock bottom and I need to get this man out of my system." Clark replied. "Well of course you're aware of the fundamentals of accepting responsibility and not being in denial. So excellent job so far. I'll have you know that this is certainly not the first time I've dealt with this sort of correlation. It's challenging because you've established what we call double jeopardy because you've helped him with his issue and have also been romantically involved with the same client. Does the wife know?" "To the best of my knowledge she doesn't." "Ok I can't forbid you to see him but regardless of our academic accomplishments, I believe we should go back to the drawing board so you understand the pending chaos, then weigh the cons and pros. You're making a lot of money in this field and about to throw it away, all over some dick?" LOL! You'll lose your license and never work in this field again. I believe your blinded by reality because he is financially stabled. If he was broke your career would be a higher priority." "See that's the thing it's not about his money, it's about him being the best guy I've met in my life, and me not wanting to lose him." "Lose him? He doesn't belong to you Dr. Simmons. Are you having trouble understanding fantasy from reality? You're his mistress, his whore, his side ass. Please begin thinking rationally. He's made you no promises but he's the recipient of what we call a double gift. That's when the client is banging his therapist while still receiving treatment. Your emotional investment has turned physical because you lack self-control and being irresponsible.

Have you taken a pregnancy test?" "No but I believe that I should because I've been feeling weird the past couple of weeks." "Please do so Dr. Simmons. We'll meet here again next week same time. Her time spent with James was now limited to her receiving treatment and still having her own clients. Since she also secretly began seeing Dr. Clark, James questioned their declining time that was spent sexing each other senseless. She hadn't mentioned anything to James about her possibly being pregnant because she wanted to know for sure. It made sense to nervously wait until the end of the month to see if nature would take its place. That wasn't the case and a phone call was made to James telling him to come to her office. As usual, he arrived in minutes filled with anticipation for an escapade but she told him to "Please stop, please sit down, I have something to tell you." "What's up baby?" "My cycle is a week late. Maybe it's because I'm sexually active that's causing it to be late." He was more poised and unexpectedly replied, "Well just take a pregnancy test, there's no reason for getting all worked up for nothing and having me purchase baby clothes and having a nursery room built. That would be one cute kid." It was Dr. Simmons who now thought James was having trouble realizing fantasy from reality. "James you're still married; I can't believe you're not freaking out about this situation." "I know you probably think I'm crazy but I can't understand why people get surprised after making conscious careless decisions. Maybe if I was happy in my marriage, I would have the typical stressful response. But I don't really like my wife at this moment and this news would surely have the effects of the atomic bomb. Dr. Simmons could care less about if his wife was screwing another guy. She loved James but the possibilities of having his child under these circumstances was quite stressful. But it was stress that caused her to have a miscarriage two weeks later.

CORNELL RICHARDS

CHAPTER 10

Turn Coats

E VERYTHING WAS GOING well for James. Business was great and he had two beautiful women in his life. He was also able to finally get Steve and Dave a job on the clean-up crew for the construction company as promised. What a great friend indeed James has been to these two malingerers. Their bills were finally paid but they still were experiencing issues in the bedroom. Although the night was cut short at Roy's event, they were there long enough to confirm his greatness. James had cured their financial issues but Roy was their miracle drug. So after consulting with each other in one of the nice restaurants that James introduced them to, Steve and Dave decided to secretly attend Roy's special classes which he would be giving great advice and sex demonstrations for men. Both men paid the fee of a hundred dollars after getting their first paychecks. Sex demonstrations are routinely for women that wanted to spice up their relationships or pleasure themselves with toys but it was simple genius that Roy came up with the idea to do the same for men. When Steve and Dave entered the room that was filled with a diverse group of guys from all levels of social economic status, they quietly took a seat and waited for their messiah. "The Whipper," arrived a few minutes late struggling to carry two boxes filled with synthetic vaginas, breast and two full body dummies that catered to his black and white students. He needed no introduction but properly did so and asked everyone else to do the same. Some of the men were shy and others were filled with enthusiasm and couldn't wait to get started. The Whipper then established the rules. "Look what's said in this room, stays in this room. If I find out, and it can be proven violators will be asked to leave and you will not be issued a refund. I started this class because I wanted to simply help those in need. As you can see I'm not the best looking guy and have had my fair share of issues with women. But I always had confidence and was able to hold a great conversation, which are the keys to being successful when dating.

After I got a job as a janitor I cleaned myself up, straightened my teeth, got a new wardrobe and a new bachelor pad." Steve then discretely asked Dave, "How many times do you think Stephany has been over there?" Dave just smiled while shaking his head and continued to focus on Roy. "This is a collaboration effort but a fun environment as well. We'll meet here once a week at 5:30 pm on Wednesdays. If you're going to be late or can't make it, just shoot me an email. Ok let's see who has some confidence and would like to share some of their horror stories. Some of the guys openly admitted that they had been experiencing bad sex since high school which left them scorned and timid. One guy, who was catholic admitted that he was so terrible that he even confessed to the priest in hopes of relief. LOL! Others mentioned that after their girlfriends viciously expressed their frustration they simply stopped dating and just decided to be celibate. A white guy who appeared to be in his mid-thirties sat in the back of the room introduced himself as "Simon." He managed to turn heads by admitting "You're my last hope because I was about to off myself." The men understood the severity of the class and James told Simon that he made a great choice in deciding to attend the group. Simon then received a few pats on the back from other classmates. James then asked, "How many married men do we have in attendance?" Half of the men rose their hands. "Ok, for the men that are married, how many of your wives don't know that you're taking this class?" Only several of the men rose their hands. The sessions that Steve and Dave were taking with Dr. Simmons had ended. Steve's domestic case was dismissed and Dave was one of the several guys that raised his hand when Roy asked, "How many of their wives didn't know that they were taking the class?" Roy took a quick note. There was a total of thirty men and the class was at full capacity. "Ok cool, I'm sure everyone here knows what a vagina and breast looks like so the next class we're going to get started. I would like to thank everyone for coming and to drive home safely."

On Wednesday evening, Roy was on time with all the goodies. Everyone was excited to get started and he separated the classroom in half by asking the married men to sit on one side of the class and the single guys to sit on the other. Group A would be for the married guys and Group B would be for the guys that were single. He then gave the married group the black and white dummies so they could have their pick when demonstrating. Roy then explained to the married group. "You know sometimes it's not about sexual intercourse, at times a woman just wants to be caressed. So let's begin with a little role playing and putting away our own urges and catering to our wives after she's had a long day of work. Group B since you guys are single I need you to simply observe and take notes. Ok, who would like to be our first volunteer?" They were reluctant until Roy mentioned, "Come on guys, you paid your money and there are some marriages hanging by a thread, so there's certainly no time to be shy." Dave discreetly said to Steve, "I certainly don't want this guy sleeping with my wife," and raised his hand to volunteer. LOL! He selected the black dummy and proceeded to rub her feet after a long day. Roy told him, "This gesture could be made after she takes a shower so she'll be more relaxed. You can also offer lotion or oil after her shower, I'm sure she wouldn't want you touching her sweaty feet. You can do so with a full body massage." Dave then massaged the dummies back and then Roy asked him, "Now I would like for you to be honest, are you a little turned on?" Dave answered with a smile "Hell yeah, I'm ready to go." Everyone laughed but Roy stated "This is a crucial point to having better sex. Having self-control. The secret is doing all of the little things that will make you and your partner want more. Women are not the only ones with the power to be a tease. That's why they say it always takes two to tangle. You've never heard of a woman teasing herself, that's insane. If we can learn how to control our urges, then we completely dominant there's. "Wow," one of the guys said, "That was really heavy, you actually make not having sex sound really cool." "Thank you."

Roy then thanked Dave for participating and asked were there any questions from either group? One guy asked, "So what happens if we have erectile dysfunction?" Roy answered, "If you have erectile dysfunction, then you're in the wrong room." There was some snickering as Roy continued to explain to the guy that, "You need to contact your doctor to see if your hearts healthy enough to even have sex. The side effects of those sexual enhancement drugs could kill a sabretooth. This class is for guys struggling with their performance but don't have a medical issue." Someone else asked, "So how many times can we take this class just in case we're still having trouble in the bedroom?" The class is for two months. Enrollment starts two weeks before it ends. If you're still having trouble, then feel free to re-apply. It's a first come first served and the hundred-dollar fee will not increase." How cliché, time surely flies when you're having fun. The guys were getting comfortable with one another but more importantly, not judging and being supportive. The class was originally supposed to end at 7:00pm but since they mistakenly surpassed that time Roy mentioned that they would pick up right where they left off with the second demonstration and to make sure everyone brought their vaginas. LOL! After class Steve and Dave began making new friends and ignoring James's text messages and calls requesting to hangout. They even began picking up the tab in bars where they usually hung out with James.

The next week they got right back to business. Roy briefly lectured the class about having confidence and how to stimulate themselves. "Instead of rushing into our women and just trying to receive gratification, how about we remain consistent in catering to our Goddesses. Once again it's about practicing self-control. I'm advising you to first perform oral sex on your lovers and making sure she has an explosive orgasm before entering her." Some men looked confused. "Here's the logic, if a woman has an orgasm it really doesn't matter how she received it, therefore after you enter her and if you ejaculate prematurely, she will not be so furious with you because she has also been pleased. As opposed to her not being satisfied at all and you laying there with a smile on your face because your needs were met. Not cool. You often hear women making fun of men having premature ejaculation but I recently did some research and found that in 2015 women between the ages of 21-50 on average, it takes them only several minutes to climax but yet we're the minute men. Unbelievable." He then asked everyone in the class to unwrap their vaginas and to begin softly licking on the clitoris.

They all were surprised that the vaginas had a fruity tropical flavor. After Roy licked his own raspberry flavored vagina, he asked, "Are you guys surprised that not all vaginas taste the same?" The class laughed and continued licking and sucking. He asked one guy to slow down and told another guy to speed up and to use his tongue a little more. As he walked around the room with his clip board giving instructions, Roy noticed that Simon, the guy who said he was about to kill himself was just sitting there with the vagina still in the wrapper and not participating. When Roy asked him "What's wrong?" the entire class turned around and began staring at him. Roy asked him again, "What's wrong Simon?" he answered, "I've never eaten pussy before." Another class mate, a black guy who favored the great "Mike Epps" blurted, "Man you don't know what you're missing, this shit is good," then loudly took another slurp of his vagina. LOL! Time was never permitted for one-on-one sessions which would have been less embarrassing but Simon explained, "I just never cared for it. A few women tried to force me to do it which was a complete turn-off, but the truth is, I just don't know how." Roy paused for a few seconds then ask him, "Do you like ice cream?" he answered "Yes cherry vanilla is my favorite kind." "Ok I don't usually do this but there's a store directly across the street, let's all take a ten-minute break." Only a few departed for a quick bathroom run but the majority of the class remained seated and waited with curiosity as things were certainly going to get pretty interesting. Class was now back in session, Simon returned with an ice cream cone and Roy asked him to slowly begin licking the cone as he would on a regular basis. The cone started to melt and Simon caught every drop before it completely dissolved. Roy informed him that "Your tongue motions were good and you used your lips quite well. Great job." Someone asked, "So why couldn't you tell him to do that with the vagina?" Roy explained "Mind over matter, I wanted him to first practice doing something that he loves and was more comfortable with, which would make it easier to do something he didn't care for. With more practice he will eventually perfect the method by using his favorite ice cream when blessing his lover.

But Simon continued to perform and minutes later he uttered, "There's some cherry jell oozing from my vagina," Roy was thrilled and congratulated him. "Congrats man, that means your vagina just had an orgasm." Everyone, please give Simon a round of applause. I'm proud of you." After that day Simon was in new spirits and felt as though he was ready to explore. This ugly duckling Roy was turning these lame ducks into blood thirsty wolves.

That night after class, Steve continued to gush about feeling as though he was being reinvented. Dave also felt the same but it wasn't because of him taking Roy's better sex class. He began to cut down on his drinking habits. He also learned earlier that same day, him and his wife Veronica was now expecting their first child. The guys finally put an end to dodging James and returned his calls after a couple weeks. They apologized and expressed their appreciation for getting them both jobs by treating him to dinner at one of his favorite restaurants. The entire night was filled with lies about them being extra busy with work and how ungrateful their wives have been now that they're employed. "Really sorry" Dave said, "Just didn't want to bug you with all our drama. It's always something with these women, now that we have jobs and the bills are paid the wife's complaining about me not spending anytime at home." Steve asked about Dr. Simmons and James replied, "Oh speaking of the devil," she just sent me a sexy photo wearing lingerie and laying on her desk." While downing their choice of liquor, their deception seemed to be more authentic and something didn't feel right to James. But he didn't want to spoil the night. They were his only friends and he was feeling a bit vulnerable. James knew that no matter how much drama occurred they always hooked up to chat about their problems. Especially after work. So when Dave made the excuse about his wife complaining about him not being at home, where else on earth could he have been? Steve remained quiet for the majority of the night which was clearly a red flag because he usually has a motor mouth, especially after consuming large amounts of alcohol. He was on his fourth round and then sheepishly said, "Oh would you look at the time, let me get going before the wife sends out a search party looking for me." He and Dave then squabbled about who would pay the check. "I got it," "No, I got it, "No, I got it." The waiter, a young good looking white guy sarcastically mentioned, "Hey I really don't care who pays, as long as the tip is good." LOL!

Steve paid the bill. The comment was actually a little rude but not as harsh as Dave and Steve have been towards James and trying to propitiate him with an evening out. Dave was tempted to come clean about the betrayal but couldn't look James in the eye. He knew if he told James the truth it would cause a tumbling domino effect, starting with their friendship being over, James possibly causing him to lose his job, miss out on the remaining classes, while also betraying Steve in the process. However, James did ask "Hey man, is everything ok? You don't look so well." Dave replied, "I'm a little nauseous, maybe I drank too much." All night he's been trying to feed James with poisonous lies but sadly the strawberry daiquiri and extra shot of tequila was enough to land Dave in the hospital that night for alcohol poisoning. Serves him right! See, it never pays to be the modern day Benedict Arnold. James rushed him to the hospital and made sure his friend had the best care. James then contacted his wife to inform her what happened but assured her he was fine so no need to leave the home. James then contacted Dr. Simmons and thanked her for the picture and told her what happened. She was glad to hear all went well but also had to remind him to contact his wife. He replied, "Oh yes that one, totally slipped my mind." Hahaha. He did so minutes later after the doctor returned and confirmed Dave also had food poisoning and needed to take a couple of days off from work. Dave was given some antibiotics and would be released that night. That night on the way home Dave repeatedly thanked James and was feeling so much better but still couldn't find the strength to come clean. Instead of clearing the air, he complained about possibly having to take a couple days off from work and how much money he's going to miss. But what's done in the dark would sure come to light and James subconsciously forgot about the negative vibes his friends were transferring.

CHAPTER 11

Confused

D R. SIMMONS PAYED her therapist a visit. She confirmed with Dr. Clark that she was indeed a few weeks pregnant but had a miscarriage. He was unsympathetic and replied, "Well I'll say that sure was a blessing in disguise due to the circumstances." She further admitted that her personal life was negatively affecting her work performance. "A few days ago, I had a client tell me that he was struggling with the idea whether to marry his girlfriend out of loyalty because he was not in love with her. He's a writer and she has been financially supporting him but the traditional love has not grown since they've been seeing each other for almost two years now. I struggled greatly and even asked myself was this possible to marry someone out of loyalty and not be in love with them? My response should have been for him to timely communicate his feelings towards her to see if she probably felt he same way to prevent her from being strung along. Instead I tried to figure it out and gave a poor response. The guy just looked at me like I had no clue what I was talking about then fired me." Dr. Clark continued to be insensitive but honest. "Yes Dr. Simmons this is how it starts, either your transgressions will come to light and ruin your career or your poor performance because of your transgressions will ruin your career. I would like for you to attack this issue like you're going on a diet. By the looks of you, that might be pretty hard to do LOL! But start with a seven-day program by having less and less communication with this gentleman. I was going to suggest for you to book your schedule with more clients but that would lead to exhaustion and being counterproductive. So find other hobbies that will occupy your time and begin this process slowly. This is the part in your life where you have to practice what you preach, either put up or shut up."

That same night James was putting her legs in the air and maneuvering her body in positions she never knew was possible. The only process that was taking slow was the full body massage she received and him cooking her dinner. She remained confused and during dinner she seriously mentioned that their relationship was becoming a negative distraction. "I have to get rid of you, you cost me to lose a client." He opposed that she was a positive distraction from Stephany's garbage. Dr. Simmons then mentioned how she dropped the ball with the writer that fired her and asked James if he could marry someone because of loyalty instead of love? He answered swiftly and suggested, "Hell no, If I'm not in love with a woman, then there will be no wedding. But the proper thing to do is when the writer accomplishes all is goals which were to have his books transformed into movies is to reward his support system but keep excellent communication so neither one of their feelings gets hurt during the process." His response was similar to what hers should have been and what also made James more enthralling. She jokingly replied "Ok so who's the therapist here, you or me? I can't believe that I causally told this guy to just see what happens and to explore other options. That was a typical bar room response not a professional, responsible solution like you suggested. I'm starting to suck." "Don't be so down on yourself sweetie. But it sounds like you might need a little more of my positive distractions to keep you on point. But for now try another piece of my Red Snapper. I also have made you a homemade peach pie that's keeping warm in the oven." He ended up eating almost the entire pie by himself and leaving a little piece in the fridge for her to take to work so she could be reminded of him. He didn't want to attract any suspicion by immediately taking a shower after going home three hours late, so he took one before leaving her apartment. Upon entering his driveway, he checked his cellphone and saw that his mother sent him an unusual text message that read, "Drink only the water that comes from your own well, and don't let your water flow out into the streets. Keep it for yourself, and don't share it with strangers. Be happy with your own wife. Enjoy the woman you married while you are young. She is like a beautiful deer, a lovely fawn. Let her love satisfy you completely. Stay drunk on her love, and don't go stumbling into the arms of another woman. The Lord clearly sees everything you do. The days of an eye for an eye tooth for a tooth are long gone and respectively shall never return because that notion interferes with the concept of forgiveness. The Lord watches where you go. Proverbs 5:15-21." When James opened the front door he saw Stephany standing in the living room checking the mail. He ran over to her and picked her up and held her in the air for a few seconds. Totally surprised, she asked "Why are you holding me in the air?" He answered, "I saw a Facebook posting telling people to stop worrying and lift their problems up to God." LOL! "That's funny, put me down, I have to go and check the stove because dinner is almost ready." But while he was putting her down Stephany smelled an unusual scent on James. Although he took a shower to remove the enduring scent of sex from his genitals, he never placed his clothes in the washing machine to remove the scent of Dr. Simmons perfume. But the entire house reeked of the pot roast and string beans that Stephany was preparing. It was delicious and the best meal that she ever made. During dinner it was the typical conversation in which she asked, "So did anything interesting happen today?" Moments of him drilling his battering ram into Dr. Simmons on the kitchen counter were vivid but he replied, "Just a typical day of counting money. Everyone is happy, so it's kind of boring around the office but I guess that's a good thing."

He then showed his appreciation for the well cooked meal by slipping a thousand-dollar gift card from Walmart in her palm with a kiss on the cheek and then left the table. Stephany begins to get suspicious but is distracted by thoughts of the numerous items she'll be purchasing with the gift card. She decided to call her girlfriends the next day. Coincidentally they're both off from work so Steph invites them on a shopping spree. They met at noon the next day and was fortunate that the entire store was having a forty percent discount on all items. When they decided to take a break to have lunch in the café area, Stephany mentioned that James is always fresh and clean after arriving home from work excessively late. "Although he doesn't have a rough job description, due to his extra hours of working, he should have some sort of perspiration. But he always arrives home just as he left the house, well groomed." Marcy replied, "Is there ever a time where you actually call us just to hang out? Why does every meeting have to be a therapy session with your James drama? But now that I think of it let me keep my big mouth shut because clearly we're all benefiting here." Marcy then told Janet to make sure her items were in separate bags. Janet did as she asked then Marcy's idea was to immediately begin stalking James. "Look it makes every bit of sense if he is cheating on you, but you need to make sure that's the case. Usually the way I find out if I was cheated on is when my gynecologist tells me I have a sexual transmitted disease. But you can't wait until you catch something so it's best to begin the investigation now. Janet what do you think?" "If he's going to cheat, he's going to cheat and its absolutely nothing you can do about it, don't even waste your time and energy fighting for something that's spoiled. But I can understand how curiosity will kill you. But I assure you if he is cheating, it will come to light without you having to lift a finger and go snooping around trying to catch him being deceptive as you were to him. Just have confidence and allow God to navigate this matter."

Stephany maxed out the gift card without purchasing James a pair of socks. But she would quickly be rewarded for her selfishness. When she arrived home later that evening, she was greeted by a stack of mail on the floor. It has been months since she had taken the therapy sessions with James and their account should have been closed. But when Stephany opened the letter it specified the billing statements and the number of times James continued to see Dr. Simmons without her having any knowledge of his attendance. Filled with rage she considered going straight to his job but patiently waited for him to come home. She couldn't wait to hear the load of crap that would be coming from his mouth trying to explain his reasons for keeping her in the dark. Moments later she heard him struggling to find his key and frantically opened the door. "What the hell is this?" She yelled and threw the billing statements in his face as he stood in the threshold. A few nosey neighbors passing by began to gaze, so James quickly entered and closed the door. "Calm down, you're over reacting." "Over reacting? This whole entire time you've been sneaking around just to see that bitch. You're having an affair, because if you were just going to see her for therapy, you could have easily told me that." "Well, what would you like for me to do Stephany?" "You've been practically doing the same thing our entire marriage and now that the tables have turned, all of a sudden you're the victim? Her eyes were filled with daggers but she just scrunched her face and grabbed the car keys off the table and stormed out the door. He thought she was just going to see either her girlfriends or worst, probably Roy, but Stephany madly swerved her way through the rush hour traffic on her way to Dr. Simmons office. This time the secretary was not there. Dr. Simmons had given her the day off and she was wrapping up the final minutes with a couple when Stephany burst into her office and completely exposed her.

Stephany's presence was frightening as she was not looking her best and the couple tried to leave but Stephany said, "No don't leave, I want you to hear this. Dr. Simmons is a whore, this woman has been sleeping with my husband and helped to destroy my family. You're a complete disgrace and take advantage of people." The couple eventually ran out of the office. Normally one would think, Dr. Simmons would be shaken but she stood her ground with no sympathy and issued a fierce reply after closing the door and turning the lock. The tables had turned again and Stephany became afraid when Dr. Simmons walked towards her with fire blazing in her eyes and asked "Are you surprised that another woman slept with your husband? The man that you did oh so wrong? All of a sudden you're so insecure. You're the one that screwed up. Now I have him. Do you really think that I was taking notes on your bullshit marriage? I was showing him that you were a terrible experiment gone wrong. Since the first day that he walked into my office I knew he was the one for me. So I was developing a treatment plan, showing him how to stay away from idiots like you. Get the hell out of my office and here's your money back. Trust and believe James's love is priceless. Stephany quickly tuck tail and ran out of the office. When she got back inside the car she cracked a devilish smile as she replayed the recorded conversation on her cellphone. Stephany had to be smart. Having damaging evidence of Dr. Simmons cold hearted confession was more strategic and significant than beating up on the puny white therapist. But anger was the norm so she stopped at the bar to have a drink and to think things through. She was completely focused and totally ignored the hounds who were offering their phone numbers and to buy her drinks. She thought things out diligently but remained in complete silence when returning home. It was now James who was in disarray and remained in a great state of confusion the entire night because of her silence. He was completely paranoid and uncharacteristically called his friends and began telling them what had transpired.

When he called Steve, he suggested, "Man you need to find a hotel quick. The silent treatment from a pissed off woman is never good. But why didn't you just throw away the billing statement?" "I actually forgot all about it coming to my house and of course it arrived before I got home." "Well at least Stephany got a taste of her own medicine but now what are you going to do?" "I don't know, that's why I called you." "Beats me." James just shook his head and hung up the phone. When he called Dave, there was no answer but Dave returned his call minutes later. "Hey what's up man?" "Dude, the gig is up," "What happened?" "When I came home today Stephany threw the therapy statement bill in my face. She saw all of the days and times that I secretly saw Dr. Simmons." "Oh crap, and you're still breathing? Wow maybe she isn't that pissed off and wants to forgive you." "She hasn't said a word to me" "Hmm... If you leave she'll think that you've gone to see Dr. Simmons. So just stay locked in the guest room." "I don't know man, what if she sets the house on fire while I'm locked in here." Her name isn't on the deed, she doesn't have a life insurance policy on me and we have a prenuptial agreement that entitles her to absolutely nothing, so there's nothing for her to lose." "Damn, you're right maybe you should take Steve's advice and just get the hell out of there to provide her with a cooling down period." That night, he packed a few belongings and nervously strolled passed her as she made a cup of coffee but he stopped to mention, "I think it's best for me to stay in a hotel for the next few days." She agreed with a slight nod and retreated to the couch. When he slammed the door, she called her friends and told them to pack a few bags for a sleep over. When he slammed the car door, he called Dr. Simmons and told her he'd be sleeping over for the next few days. Ha!

When the girls came over for what was actually a three-night slumber party, they sympathized with Stephany because they both were under the impression that progress was being made. All three of the ladies were football fans so during the typical shot taking and man bashing, Marcy asked Stephany, "If your relationship was a football team who would be most fitting?" Stephany answered, "Without a doubt my relationship would be the New England Patriots. Just like them, James and I have everything but we are some cheating bastards." LOL! Marcy asked Janet the same question and she answered, my marriage would have been the San Francisco 49ers because of their longevity of success and class. Janet then asked "Who would yours be Marcy?" She paused then answered, the damn Philadelphia Eagles. They're so unpredictable, and you never know what's going to come out of my mouth but watching the Eagles play, and listening to me talk you always feel like you're about to have a heart attack. They all were dying with laughter as Marcy drank the last bit of Brandy. On the other end Dr. Simmons gave James a refill of wine and made him a second Healthy Choice TV dinner. Although James's relationship remained in shambles, everyone else's was thriving. His parents snuggled under each other comfortably, Stephany's parents slept well, Dave was implementing his new found techniques on his wife Veronica, and Steve and Carrie couldn't be more thrilled to remain being married which he also utilized his new lessons. The tables had turned once AGAIN in favor of Stephany. After their heavy drinking, both Marcy and Janet went to bed early leaving Stephany to contemplate whether to stay with James or finally decide to move on and find happiness elsewhere. Neither James or Stephany had called to check on each other but providing Stephany with some time to herself was an excellent psychological strategy. He knew that she wouldn't stay in the house by herself so it was well anticipated that the girls would be there. But they provided no help whatsoever and Stephany was confident that James would come crawling back to her. He needed TO BE TAUGHT A LESSON. When James finally did return begging for her forgiveness she would propose what everyone thought was the most preposterous suggestion that only a fool would submit to such a request.

CHAPTER 12

Big Decision

IT WASN'T THE case of the 80/20 rule with James and Dr. Simmons as depicted in the classic Tyler Perry film, "Why did I Get Married," where one of the male characters left his wife because she was only 80% satisfying, then sought a replacement that seemed to be more appealing but turned out to be 20% adequate. Dr. Simmons was the real deal. She was understanding, a sports fan, drop dead gorgeous, but a mediocre cook just like Stephany. But that wasn't an issue because compared to James, everyone else's cooking was mediocre. It was the case of picking platinum or gold between the two Queens. Stephany was his wife and they clearly had a history of ups and downs during their brief marriage. Dr. Simmons was a new spark that brought the 4th of July every time they spent time together in or outside of the bedroom. The fear of the unknown was enchanting and made the decision to finally cut off Dr. Simmons more difficult. James knew that marriage was a job and during this time he couldn't look himself in the mirror and say he was doing a great job. He couldn't tell himself or others in his circle that he had done everything humanly possible to make his marriage work. So these unfulfilled sentiments fueled James's fire to have a successful marriage. And of course a thriving thirty plus- year marriage from his parents played a significant role in deciding to stay and work things out with Stephany. But would that fire be extinguished after having their first face to face meeting since James left the house? It was late in the afternoon when he called home and began his heart felt speech that turned into rambling but what was enough to earn him a meeting in his living room. Stephany had cleaned the house thoroughly, and was evocatively dressed and covered with the most riveting scents from Bath & Body Works. The fire place was comfortably lit and she offered him a glass of Strawberry Sangria which was accepted. After his second glass Stephany watched him carefully as he uttered the words, "I WOULD DO ANYTHING TO GET YOU BACK."

She took a sip of her glass, which she had the same choice of drink and took a deep breath then replied "Ok James, up until this point you've always been a man of your word, so I'm going to hold you to that. I am willing to stay married and COMMITTED to you under one condition." He instantly became excited and desperate, "Anything, anything you name it, and it's done." "Ok James if you would like to stay married, I would like for you to go and receive sex lessons from Roy." BOOMM!! The steam from James's ears was enough to dowse the fireplace. She slightly back peddled in fear of him launching himself and slitting her throat with the bottle opener. "Are you out of your mind? Now you're just trying to take advantage of my vulnerability. You're a piece of crap." "James, James, please listen to me. I'm telling you that this could work. Please just lower your ego and see the good that can come from the bad. You're just ashamed about what others will think. God is telling me that this could save our marriage. I know this sounds crazy but if you can honestly say to yourself that, if the shoe was on the other foot, and you weren't happy with my sex, would you honestly turn down the opportunity, if I agreed to bring another woman in our bedroom?" The question caused him to have brain freeze. "Damn, she had a point." She continued pressing him, "So if your answer is yes that you would accept bringing another woman into our bedroom, don't you think it's less painful for you to sit in a classroom? As it relates to learning in a classroom and our infidelity, two negatives equals a positive result." That was the dagger as James paced around the living room and couldn't believe he was actually considering this craziness. He didn't give her an answer that night because he was still upset. He called his parents the next day and told them Stephany's bright idea. His father said, "Well I'm not really surprised, that's the kind of crap you kids are into nowadays. When I was a kid," before his father could finish, James hung up the phone. He then called Stephany's parents. They became annoyed with James and thanked him for all that he had done for them but politely told him that they were not getting involved. Stephany still loved James but her parents thought she was just making another bad resolution for her issues. When James called Dave, Dave admitted, "Man she has a point. It may sound like manipulation, but maybe some good could come out of you going. God works in mysterious ways."

CORNELL RICHARDS

James was a bit surprised that he took Stephany's side and the suspicious feelings returned that James felt the night at the bar, when Dave had to be rushed to the hospital. But James summed up his feelings that Dave was just being fare. While having lunch with the girls, Stephany mentioned her master plan to reel James back in perfectly trained. Marcy replied, "So let me get this straight, "Instead of immediately divorcing your husband because you found out he cheated on you. You want him to get sex lessons from the guy you had an affair with. Janet this is one crazy Bitch. A table of younger white females overheard Marcy and chimed in. "Oh my God, I think that's incredible, "one said. "Yeah that's insane, hopefully if my brain cells aren't fried by the time I reach your age, I will be able to come up with some crazy shit like that," another stated. Janet asked, "So what if he doesn't do well in the course?" Before Stephany could answer, Marcy blurted, "Wow you've certainly made things more interesting. Forget about him not doing well in the class, I really want to see if James is stupid enough to actually go through with this." Stephany answered, "Marcy please don't take this lightly, if James wants to have me back, then this is what's required. I tried it the right way by going to counseling and clearly he and the therapist were working pretty hard together. Now, we'll do it my way. Or it's over.

A few days later, the classes that Dave and Steve were taking had finally ended and both men decided to celebrate at a local bar in the city. Although James was still in the dark about them taking Roy's sex class, Dave asked James to come along for a few drinks because he knew his friend could use some company. While having a few beers and toasting, "To the good life," both Dave and Steve was careful not to spill the beans. But as it turned out, Dave was more reckless before the party even started. Dave mistakenly brought along the certificate for completing Roy's sex class. While rambling about how much of a great friend and how much love he had for James, the certificate slipped out of his jacket and fell on the floor without Dave noticing it. James picked it up, slipped it into his back pocket, and continued laughing and smiling, then went into the bathroom to get a better look at the certificate where he could clearly see CERTIFICATE OF COMPLETEION PRESENTED BY ROY "THE WHIPPER." The moment was nothing short of Robert the Bruce betraying the great William Wallace in the classic film "Braveheart." Besieged with temporary insanity, the weird vibes, the two-week silent treatment, the moments of Dave vouching for Roy, and Dave taking Stephany's side all made sense. Dave then entered the bathroom, "Hey, there you are my good man," James then sucker punched Dave and he stumbled against the wall. James then threw the certificate at him and asked, "What the hell is this? You damn snake." He hit Dave again and tried to strangle him but Steve came into the bathroom and broke up the fight but was also the recipient of the thrashing. When some other patrons entered the restroom, James fled but not before throwing a hundred-dollar bill at the bar tender.

He went home that night, and sat on the couch with Stephany icing his bruised hands. This was obviously a huge setback for their marriage and for a few minutes, Stephany was rightfully discouraged. But like a flip of a switch, she turned and said, "You know what this means right?" "Yes, I know what this means, it means that my life sucks and no one is to be trusted. All the people that I'm showing love to are traitors." She stared at him to see if he could comprehend without her speaking but he failed due to anger. "James, this is confirmation that Roy is the real deal, you might not want to admit it but your friends are not traitors, they didn't want to hurt your feelings. They were in desperate need of help to enhance their marriage so they secretly took the classes and see, they're all happy couples. I'm asking you to dig deep in your soul and realize that we all truly love you James. We've all made terrible decisions but we're all doing something to help better the lives of others. The sole purpose of Roy's class is to help people. Your friends were seeking help, so what does it matter where the help came from as long as they become a better individual and remain married." That was another great point. But James wasn't completely sold and a few days later, he and Stephany watched Roy's popularity get aired on the evening news. To add insult to injury, Dave and Steve were posing for pictures with Roy as he announced them as his honor students. Stephany just looked at James and shook her head then walked away. It was at that moment when he knew that his friendship with Dave and Steve had to be restored and a collaboration with Roy was a necessity.

Stephany actually called and arranged the meeting with Dave and Steve to come to the house. Both men were thrilled to hear from her and wasted no time arriving the very next day after work. They were a bit apprehensive, but when they arrived Stephany had prepared dinner for the gentlemen and left the trio alone to reconcile their differences. They were extremely apologetic towards James and avowed what Stephany said in regards to their motive of taking Roy's class. Subsequently, apprehensiveness turned to comfort and Steve began to rave about Roy. "Man this guy is the truth, he's like a sex messiah." My wife can't get enough of me." Dave emphasized with James because his situation was far more sensitive and shockingly embarrassing because James had to go to the ugly man who slept with his wife for sex lessons. LOL! Steve suggested for James to not even reveal himself and to just suck up all the knowledge but Dave opposed and explained that James had to reveal himself because authenticity throughout the entire process was vital. "Furthermore, what if you don't expose who you are and you guys become friends and he secretly tells you about a woman he's been with and shows you pictures and the woman turns out to be your wife? That wouldn't be good." "Great point," Steve said. Dave continued, "If you in fact decided to go through with this, it would truly be a courageous act and a testament for your love for Stephany. We're cheering for you, but I'm curious to know, what will you do if this doesn't work? Self-control is clearly a main focal point in order to acquire what Steve said earlier about sucking up all the knowledge. The point that I'm trying to make is, as soon as you walk into the classroom and become face to face with the troll that slept with your wife, you could immediately snap out and kill this man." James answered, "If the relationship cannot be repaired divorce will be imminent and we'll part amicably. But you're correct, it has been mentally pestering about my initial reaction upon meeting this guy. Self-control is crucial." As Stephany collected their dirty plates off the table, Steve congratulated her on a job well done with the half chicken, mash potatoes, broccoli, and string beans. She replied that it was courtesy of Boston Market. LOL!

Stephany quickly placed the dirty dishes in the dishwasher and planned to head straight to her room but paused at the top of the stairs to ease drop as the men continued their dialogue. Unfortunately, they lowered their voices so she couldn't hear clearly when James made the final decision whether or not to go through with her plan. She only heard them saying how happy they were to being friends again and wishing him the best with everything. When the door slammed she ran into the bathroom and took a shower then finally went to bed. James finally flopped on the couch watching the ESPN high lights. He finally made up his mind what he wanted to do right before drifting off to sleep. The next morning, Stephany jumped out of bed like a child on Christmas ready to open gifts. James was already at the table having a cup of lemon tea and staring out the window. "Good morning honey. So how did it go with Dave and Steve last night?" He adamantly replied, "Never mind Dave and Steve, you're my wife and you started all of this garbage. I've decided that you're a reckless peace of shit, pack what little belongings you have and get the hell out of my house now before I call the police." Standing there stunned, she finally woke up out of what was a nightmare. It felt so real but when she went down stares James was at the table drinking a hot cup of lemon tea and staring out the window. She said "Good morning honey, so how did it go last night with Dave and Steve?" His reply was obstinate, "Never mind Dave and Steve you're my wife and I've decided to continuing fighting for this marriage because I love you. It will be tough but I'll set aside my ego and do what's necessary to save our marriage. I just need to know that you're in this with me 100% no screwing around this time or it's over."

She threw herself into his arms and promised him with a kiss. Her morning breath never tasted so good and she asked, "Ok so when will we get started? Would you like for me to contact Roy or you'll do it?" "I got this baby." Later that day Steph met up with Janet and Marcy to tell them the good news. Janet was proud to hear that James decided to fight for the marriage but Marcy was dying with laughter. "Wow Steph I'm proud of you to, I have to admit, I never really thought that you would pull it off." Two younger Caucasian females that sat across from them having lunch bravely chimed in. "Wow that sounds amazing, congrats." The other young lady who was clearly high on marijuana said "Now, I really want my brains cells to be fried so I can only think of crazy shit like that." LOL. Steph thanked the ladies and mentioned to her friends that although James agreed, she was struggling to decide whether to give Roy a heads up that he would be contacted by her husband. Both Janet and Marcy was torn because since James did agree to take the classes, her giving him a heads up shouldn't be a problem. So she contacted Roy that same evening and gave him the heads up that James would be enrolling in one of his classes. Of course he was shocked when seeing her email but more surprised after reading her message. He replied, "Hey I don't think that's a good idea. I'm doing extremely well and don't need any drama. He can find help elsewhere, a matter of fact, thank you for letting me know because I'll make sure to erase his name once it appears on my enrollment chart." "She replied pleading with him and he began to flirt by asking, "Well, what's in it for me?" She sternly replied, "Look we had our fun Roy and I'm exhausting every option before I divorce this man. I want to be able to say that I did everything humanly possible to make this marriage work. You'd be doing us a huge favor." "Ha, trouble in paradise I see, ok ok. I'll think about it but no promises."

CHAPTER 13

The Work

WITH ALL THE media attention that Roy was getting and the confirmation from his friends along with the stinging truth from his wife that Roy was the savior of their marriage. James was confident that all would be well but brought along Dave and Steve for moral support, when meeting Roy. He asked them to wait in the car on that cold winter evening. Stephany had never specified an exact time her husband would be contacting Roy. So that evening as Roy struggled to find his keys which mistakenly fell under his desk. After he managed to retrieve them and looked up, the commanding presence of James Pain slowly entered the threshold. Roy asked "May I help you with something?" James turned directly to him then glanced around the room before answering "Yes, yes you can. Would you mind telling me the pleasure you get from ruining marriages if your job is to help save them?" Roy replied, "Excuse me and who may I ask are you?" "I'm James Pain, Stephany's husband," "Oh James, I was actually expecting you, sorry we had to meet under these conditions." "Wait a minute, what do you mean you were expecting me?" "Well Steph called and told me you were interested in taking the class." James continued to be macho. "First of all, her name is Stephany or Mrs. Pain to you. And I'm not interested in anything this was her idea." "Ok, I understand. But hey, look I guess you're off the hook because my next two classes are filled, so thanks for stopping by." James's expressions immediately changed, "Woe, woe, woe, wait a minute. What do you mean the classes are filled?" "Yeah, the next availability is next year, but you can reserve your seat now if you'd like." The macho grand entrance James had made turned into desperation acts of ass kissing. "But I don't have another year to wait, Steph and I need help now and I promised her I would do this. It's the last resort to saving our marriage, you have to squeeze me in." But Roy was also quite stern. "Look, I'm terribly sorry but I have rules and regulations to follow as well, and I can't accept any more students, its state law. Thirty students, that's the max."

Roy then closed his briefcase, thanked James for coming by and tried to walk out on him but James grabbed him by the arm and said, "Look I really need your help." James then cracked a smile and said, "I'm just messing with you, there's plenty of room in the next class." Roy continued laughing as James was also relieved but stated, "Too soon bro for the jokes, way too soon for the jokes." "Got it, but the new classes start next week, I'll see you there." "Yup, I'll be there, thank you." Both men then shook hands and departed in different directions. When James went back to his car, he was looking furious. "What's wrong?" Steve asked, "Did you guys get into a fight? Because that's the same look you had on your face after you kicked our ass in the bathroom." "No we didn't, it's cool. But I strictly told Stephany not to contact him and inform him that I was coming. He said that she called him." Dave understood his annoyance but suggested, "Man don't even say anything to her. She probably just got excited and wanted to make sure you would be taking the class. The most important thing is you got in and certainly won't regret it." As soon as James got home he confronted Stephany while she laid on the couch. "What part of not to contact Roy didn't you understand? See you're going behind my back already." "OK, ok, you're right. Look I was just really anxious for you to get started." His anger was calmed because of her cute puppy dog face. He replied, "Look, this entire process is about trust. So I need you to trust me when I say that I'm going to do more than my best in this class because my best might not be good enough." She was thrilled to hear him speak so forcefully, but was surprised to see her weight had stayed the same after weeks of working out.

Her svelte frame had become curved with intense cravings but once again unnoticed by James.

A week later she stepped on the scale and waited on the results for her pregnancy test. It wasn't a financial issue that she feared because her child support payments would double her paychecks. She was more concerned about who the biological father was. So after counting the pounds her body was gaining, she counted the weeks that she last slept with Roy because around that time she and James had a failed attempt at make-up sex. What is a woman supposed to do when make-up sex isn't good? The timing couldn't be any perfect for her to bring this to James's attention. The pregnancy test confirmed she was in fact expecting which her gynecologist determined she was one month pregnant. She immediately became paranoid and stressed whether or not to tell James. Once again she consulted with her girlfriends and Janet mentioning, that, "Honesty was the best policy. If you hide this from James regardless if the baby belongs to him, you will not be trusted in his eyes because once again you're hiding information." Marcy coached, "Don't tell James a damn thing until after he takes the class. He'll probably do well and you don't want to ruin your chances of knowing what great sex feels like with your husband because he'll leave you. So basically you've made him more equipped for another woman to reap the benefits of all that you've been through." Janet replied to Marcy, "You're sick." But Marcy continued, "I really feel bad for you, that you possibly got pregnant from bad sex. Not that I'm hoping the baby belongs to Roy, but it would have been nice if you could say that you actually enjoyed making your child." Janet wasted no time correcting Marcy's idiotic views. "What would have been really nice, is if she kept her legs closed and this foolishness wouldn't have happened. I really don't feel bad for either of you, because neither of you value marriage. Your generation just goes with the flow and then sends a text message." LOL!

Stephany took a huge gamble and didn't tell her husband that she could possibly be pregnant for another man. Overall, everything was going according to plan. James had begun taking the classes which the first day reminded him of his childhood jitters. He hasn't been this nervous about going to school since being bullied in the 3rd grade. His nervousness got the best of him. The first week of taking the sex classes, he did poorly. He was out of zone, made others feel uncomfortable and too analytical when answering questions. One student joked about James possibly having to need a tutor. The look that James gave his classmate quieted the entire room and the jokester felt like a pray ready to be devoured at the sound of the bell. But there was no confrontation between the two men. James cordially asked for some respect and informed the frightened man that he was getting too comfortable. The guy apologized but then Roy asked to speak with James in private after class. "Look thanks for being such a classy guy about this, and that guy had no right to say that to you. BUT he was right, I think you might need a tutor because you're just not getting it. I think the pressure of knowing that Steph, I mean Mrs. Pain and I had an affair is starting to weigh on you. James you don't have anything to prove. Try dressing a little more causal to help you loosen up. Just relax and let the answers flow naturally. The next class we'll focus on finding a woman's spot and not having sex. A definite oxymoron but should be pretty interesting. The following day, James arrived with Apple Fritters and coffee for the entire class. Half of the class had not eaten all day and the other half was very drowsy so the coffee was right on time and even Roy enjoyed an apple fritter.

How weird it must have been to serve refreshments to the man that slept with his wife. But James was the man of the hour as everyone expressed their appreciation for the kind gesture. "Man that hit the spot," one of the students said. Roy stated, "Well imagine how your significant other would feel if you constantly hit her spot, just like that coffee and apple fritter was surely fulfilling." "Today we'll be discussing how to locate your partners spot and then not having sex at all." "Wait a minute," one student said, I thought you were supposed to be helping us have better sex, now you're teaching abstinence, I knew this was a scam and too good to be true." The guy then jumped up and began packing his belongings to leave. But James said, "Wait a second, let's hear him out, I'm sure he's not charging a hundred dollars just to tell us not to have sex." The guy then sat back down and Roy thanked James and proceeded with the lesson. "Now normally after caressing a woman's vagina, she would be in the mood. But statistics have shown that 85% of women have a spot above the waist line that really puts them in the mood. This is where Active Communication comes into play. Active Communication is asking your partner questions while exploring and massaging the body. How does that feel? Do you like that? Am I rubbing too hard? Where does it ache the most so I can concentrate on that area? During this time your partner usually would reveal the spot on her body that's most pleasurable." One student raised his hand and said, "That's some really great information, I really didn't know that. I thought all women had the same spot." "Thank you, Roy replied. But here is the fun part. Now that you have been notified by your partner about the location of her trigger area, simply caress and cuddle with her but establish self-control and do not have intercourse at that moment.

But the very next time the heat of passion arrives, you gently or if she prefers it rough, you rub that area while having intercourse or performing oral sex. This is what causes a woman to have an explosive orgasm." While taking notes James couldn't help picturing this rodent sucking and slobbering all over his beautiful wife. Roy's graphic instructions of listening to your partner during intercourse was infuriating. "When penetrating, if she says harder, harder, you do as she request. Do not do what feels better to you. It's her moment and totally your responsibility to make sure she is satisfied." Perhaps Roy got a little carried away during his sermon and had a poor choice of words. "Trust and believe it's your responsibility to make sure that she is satisfied because whatever you don't do, another man will." The top flew off the steaming kettle as James jumped up and stormed out of the room. Everyone was confused but one guy felt the vibe. Jerry, a slender built white mid-age fair looking male who wore glasses, knew something fishy was going on when Roy asked to speak with James privately. James clearly needed to catch some air but he ended up missing the remaining time in class. He stood outside the building as everyone departed and Jerry walked over, politely introduced himself and said, "I think this belongs to you." He then gave James his coat and leather messenger bag then said, "You know, I can tell you're a different type of guy that can appreciate someone being blunt, So I'll tell you the truth. This instructor is a piece of shit. I don't like him, he slept with my wife." Blown away at Jerry's disclosure James replied, "Wait a minute he slept with your wife to?" Yup, I never sought help for my sex issues so my wife sought help for me but forgot to tell me." James cracked a smile at his humor.

Jerry continued, "My wife was the one who inspired him to become an instructor." James interrupted "No, I think my wife was the one to inspire him." Jerry disagreed, "No I think my wife was the one, she's pretty good at manipulation but I tried to kill her after she offered me the ridiculous ultimatum. Luckily I beat the attempted murder charge but they found me guilty for aggravated assault and of course a restraining order was enforced. After three years in the big house I came home and thought about getting remarried but didn't want to bring the same problem into the future so when I heard he was having the class, I said what the hell? And signed up." James replied, "Bravo to you for wanting to better yourself but I still have to look at this chick every day." "I still look at my ex every day to. She was beautiful, had a great job, very sarcastic and just full of life. I certainly didn't mind a little chocolate mixed with my cream," and then the unthinkable happened.

Jerry took out a picture of his ex-wife and showed it to James. "Here she is." James was able to compose his expression when seeing the beautiful photo of Marcy. Jerry mentioned, "Boy she sure was something." James gave his approval with a grin and a nod. Jerry continued "But where ever she is, I hope she's happy, I've moved on and hold no grudges. Just look at it this way James, when this class is over, you'll be able to patch things up with your wife and remain a happily married man." James nodded again and said, "Yeah that's basically what it comes down to. Well I should get going, it was nice chatting with you Jerry. I'll see you next week?" "Likewise James, I'll see you next week."

On the way home, the feeling was bitter sweet from the information James had received. His case could finally be proven of how Stephany's BFF was no good but what also would be another dose of betrayal from his wrong doings along with Marcy's. That wasn't a good category to be in but Steph needed to hear the truth. When he entered the driveway she was sweeping off the steps. "Hey sweetie, come inside," he said. "What's wrong?" she presumed. She continued "Look if it's about the class, I know it's tough but you're doing an amazing job and it's going to pay off." "Thank you, the class is fine overall, great stuff but this friend of yours Marcy is a reptile. Did you know that she also slept with Roy? From what I was told by her ex-husband who's also taking the class, she inspired Roy to be an instructor." "This is insane, are you telling me that my best friend and I had an affair with the same guy and she never told me and have been pretending this entire time not to know who he is?" "That's exactly what I'm saying. Then the ex-husband showed me pictures of him and Marcy but I didn't say that I knew her and that you guys were friends." "Yeah that would have been pretty awkward." "He did some time for aggravated assault after finding out about the affair. If I had known him during that time, I would have sent him some money because he deserved to be compensated for his services. Marcy cheated on her husband with Roy then told her husband to get sex instructions from him, sounds like birds of a feather flock together." "Oh come on James. Please we've come too far, so don't make this about me and you." "Ok, yes you're right. So what are you going to do about this Marcy chick?" Stephany just sat down and took a deep breath. James suggested "I say you pretend to continue being in the dark and simply cut her off without a notice and if she comes to the house, mistakenly shoot her thinking she was a burglar." "Funny how that was also my first thought. Hahaha, wow we do make a great team. However, you just continue to do well in the class. This was obviously a curve ball to cause a distraction and I'm not going to let it ruin our progress. You just continue to be in the dark with her ex-husband having any knowledge of your affiliation and I'll handle Marcy." "Ok, sounds like a plan, hey I'm sorry this really has to be a little rough for you to. Are you alright, you don't look so good." "I'm just a little dehydrated, can you please get me some water?" As Stephany sat waiting for James to return with the glass of water, Marcy sent her a text message mentioning how much she valued their friendship and that Stephany was a huge inspiration. Steph just sipped the glass of water and replied back with a smiley face.

CHAPTER 14

The Beef

STEPHANY WAS CONFIDENT that neither Marcy or Janet had any plans after work the next day, and if so they would instantly change them if she showed up wanting to hang out and that's exactly what happened. They actually had plans to work overtime at the hospital but when Stephany called, Janet and Marcy immediately blew off the extra funds and decided to meet in the city. "Hey girl," "Hey my two favorite ladies." They were immediately seated in a classy bistro and given menus. Marcy quickly established, "Hey this is my treat." Now normally, Steph was a modest eater, but this time she ordered almost everything on the menu out of spite. "Wow, those munchies are really kicking in," Janet teased. It was just Stephany's way of sprinkling her frustration before exploding. When the food arrived Steph only took a bite of the four entrees she ordered and mentioned that she wasn't really hungry. When the nice waiter asked, "Would you like a box for those leftovers?" Steph said, "No thanks, you can just throw it all away." Marcy snapped, "Bitch what the hell is going on with you?" The waiter ran away, leaving them to squabble. "No, you're the bitch, do you mind explaining why you've been pretending this whole entire time not to know who Roy is? Marcy looked confused, "What?" but Janet was even more baffled and said "What are you talking about Stephany?" "I'll show you what I'm talking about." Steph then pulled out the photo of Jerry and Marcy and threw the picture onto the middle of the table." Remarkably while Jerry was rambling about his breakup, James quickly snapped a photo of his picture with Marcy. Marcy picked up the picture from off the table and was speechless. "Now you tell us, who the hell are you, because clearly I have no idea who you are." Janet turned to Marcy and ask "Are you serious?" Marcy struggled to find the words to justify her zany display of great friendship.

She eventually confessed and admitted to feeling jealous when Stephany bragged about Roy. "I certainly didn't want a man to come between me and my best friend so I didn't say anything. It was clearly the wrong decision but it's not like we were sleeping with him at the same time." Janet asked, "Well we don't know, we're you?" "No, I wasn't." Steph asked, "So how come you never told us you were married?" "I divorced Jerry right before I got the job at the hospital. I just wanted a fresh start and to forget about the whole thing and I got that fresh start when I met you two. It was a brief marriage, less than a year. "He turned out to be an asshole and was terrible in the bedroom. That's when I met Roy in a bar here in the city. I was so drunk, the only thing I remember is how he umm… The waiter returned and asked would they like the bill. Marcy told him to, "Relax cutie pie we're going to be here for a while. A matter of fact can you bring me a shot of 1800 vodka?" Janet said, "Well what the hell, I'm going to need one to." The waiter quickly disappeared to grant their request. Marcy carried on, "I'm really sorry Steph, you were already going through enough." Steph was unsympathetic but was careful not to cause too much stress. "No I can't accept that. Men lie, women lie, but friends don't lie to each other." Marcy then got fed up with the ass kissing. "Look bitch, I told you it was a mistake, and you're calling me a liar?" Well we'll see who's the liar when I tell James that you might be pregnant by Roy and you've been keeping it a secret. If you're lucky, we'll see you back at the time clock instead of living the good life." Marcy gulped her shot of 1800 vodka, payed the bill then stormed out of the restaurant.

That did not go as planned and Stephany found herself in an even bigger predicament. An intoxicated Janet said, "Well I'm not pregnant, even though some days I sit and wish I had been. But I don't think Marcy is going to say anything, that woman is just running her mouth like she always does." "I don't know Janet, I never saw this coming and she also had a look in her eye that I've never seen before." "Well go after her and apologize, it's certainly not worth losing James for, if anyone should tell him that you're pregnant by someone else, it should be you." By the time Steph ran over to the door in attempt to catch Marcy walking down the street, she was out of sight. Steph sent her a text but there was no reply. Stephany then made sure Janet got home safely by providing door to door service but her ride back to New Town Square was vexing. On the other hand, during her ride home Marcy began her plot to destroy Stephany with one simple phone call. She knew James already didn't care too much for her and this would be a perfect opportunity to get on his good side. That night when she got settled in, Marcy called James from a block number but hung up the phone when he answered. After building up the courage to finally go through with trying to ruin her friend, she called again but hung up the phone. Stephany had also reached home and James mentioned, "Someone was playing on the phone. Every time I said hello I could hear them breathing and they just hung up." Stephany was scared and completely paranoid. "Hey I just wanted to say whatever happens at the end of the classes I'm still going to love you, I'm truly sorry for all that I've done to hurt you James." He also apologized and gave her a kiss as the phone rang again but this time someone answered. It was Dr. Simmons telling him how much she missed him and she couldn't believe he had chosen to be with Stephany. "I thought I was a big girl James and could move on without you, it's been months and I'm still seeing a therapist and trying to get over you."

"Well keep seeing him, nothing or no one is going to come between me and my wife." And he hung up the phone. Stephany thanked him for standing his ground but the phone rang again and this time Stephany answered it. Marcy said, "I don't want to talk to you, put your husband on the phone." Steph replied laughing, "Hey girl, no just relaxing." "Marcy said, oh ok since you want to play stupid, I'll play stupid right along with you and contact him at his job tomorrow. Sleep well." When Stephany hung up the phone James asked, "So how did it go with that fool Marcy?" "That was actually her trying to hook up for lunch tomorrow." James said, "I would love to feed her to the Taliban for lunch but they probably wouldn't want her. But anyway you set her straight honey, just like I just did with Simmons." He kissed her then went to bed. Surprisingly, Steph didn't have any trouble going to sleep but the morning sickness kicked in which she pretended to be defecating and told James to use the other bathroom. Time was running out. James had only a couple more weeks of class and she had developed a baby bump. Steph spent the day updating her resume, looking at a few apartments in the city and planned on being a single mother. When James returned home from work that evening, nothing appeared to happen because he would have been furious if Marcy had actually called him. Steph finally had made up her mind to tell James what was going on but waited until he got settled. He laid on the couch and she began to walk over to him but the house phone rang. She ignored the first ring and was going to totally ignore the call but when she saw Janet's name appear she stopped and answered. "Hey kiddo" Janet said, thanks for dropping off an old lady last night." "No problem, that's what friends are for." "Hey kiddo, someone else is on the phone and they need to speak with you." Steph already had a clue who it was, who else could it have been? It was a three-way call and Marcy answered. "Hey Steph, I know you're pissed but I just wanted to apologize, God knows the last thing you need is anymore drama and I'm sorry for the things I said and playing on your phone."

"Steph was relieved, and quickly walked away from James and lowering her voice before replying to Marcy. "It's ok, I take the blame for that spat. It was a terrible coincidence. You did sincerely apologize but at the time, that wasn't good enough for me and I over did it." Janet chimed in, "Don't be too hard on yourself Steph. I told that fool that she went way too far by calling and disrespecting your home." Marcy answered, "Ok and I agreed to squash it because that's my girl and she has bigger fish to fry. Steph I got your back if the baby isn't his and James puts you out. I'll work some extra overtime at the job to give you some money to help get an apartment." Janet second that notion, "Yeah me to Steph so stop worrying, just come clean and tell James the truth." "Oh girls thank you so much." By the time Stephany hung up the phone James grabbed her by the throat. He had gotten up off the couch and went upstairs to listen to her conversation on the other phone, and heard everything. "You bitch, lying again, you're still friends with Marcy and possibly pregnant with another man's child. This marriage just keeps getting better and better." He squeezed harder until a knock at the door caused him to loosen his grip. It was a pizza delivery Marcy had paid for and had sent to their home as a piece offering. James was scared and thought Stephany would run out of the house screaming for help. She coughed while rubbing her throat for relief. But when Steph closed the door he thought, maybe he should be the one running out of the house screaming for help from the look on her face. He maintained a good distance when ordering her to, "Get out." She confidently replied, "I'm not going anywhere, you're going to sit your ass down and have a slice of pizza." "What? Bitch are you crazy?" "No, I'm being cordial. Look this is bad and a huge psychological setback. You have every right to be upset. But if you would have gotten Dr. Simmons pregnant, I would have stayed with you. The only way that we're not going to be together is if you divorce me or until death do us apart. I'm unsure if this child is yours and wasn't going to tell you until after the class was over because I wanted you to have a clear head.

The main agenda was to have you complete the class without pounding Roy's face in, so when I found out I was pregnant, I opted to do a little damage control." James squeezed his fist then tossed the pizza across the living room. That was the indication that he agreed to what she was saying. "So what about Roy? He asked. What if the baby is not mine? Since you're only a couple of months and obviously doing a damn good job of hiding the pregnancy, you could just get an abortion to end the psychological torture and we could start fresh." Steph sat there and stared at James then replied "No, I'm not aborting my child." "So wait a minute, first I agree to getting sex lessons from the guy you had an affair with, now you want me to take care of his child? You are truly something special. I sure stuck my dick in the dirt. But I will not be taken for a fool any longer." "James, I'm not taking you for a fool. This is something that should never happened. But I just said if you had gotten that whore of yours pregnant, then I would have stayed with you. Doesn't that count for something?" "Hell no, because the fact is she's not pregnant and at least I was responsible enough and pulled out?" Steph pleaded, "Once again this is a psychological set back, not something that's definite." That truth was very soothing to James but after sitting and rubbing the bridge of his nose, he said "Ok I'll be the one to tell Roy and we'll figure something out." He regretted tossing the pizza across the living room. But since all the slices had not fallen out of the box, he placed two of them in the microwave, gave her one and they sat quietly that night and ate in peace.

After the next class, it was James who asked to speak to Roy in private. "Hey James, you were a bit quiet in class today. What's on your mind?" James was fuming but remained calm when replying. "What's on my mind is, my wife is pregnant and she doesn't know which one of us is the father." Roy was frightened and lost for words. He was expecting James to say something less fatiguing but quickly toughened up and replied "Hey, you two have certainly came along way and you're making tremendous progress. Overall, you're one of the best students in the class but I strongly suggest that she get an abortion so you two can start fresh." "Yeah that's exactly what I said but she won't budge." Roy stroked his newly groomed goatee then suggested "Ok would you like for me to speak with her." "No, you won't have any direct contact with her. I'll be the mediator, you tell me your ideas and I'll go and present them to her." Roy nodded his head but disagreed. "No disrespect James, I truly think you're an incredible man and obviously well accomplished but I think we both can agree that I have a way with persuading women." James nodded and totally agreed with him and instantly changed his mind. "Ok I'll set up a meeting." But Roy disagreed "No, let's set her up. Simply take her to lunch, walk away for a significant period of time but keep a close eye on us." "Oh, I most certainly will be doing that sir." "While you're maintaining your distance, I'll be applying my magic." "Ok Roy, as long as that magic doesn't lead back to my bedroom." Roy smiled then replied, "Keep a close eye to catch the signal telling you its ok to return to the table. The signal will be, when I wipe my mouth with a napkin." I'll then disappear into thin air and by the time you return to the table, she will do as you command." How sad it was that Jerry overheard exactly the time and location for them to meet.

When both men left out of the room, James received a taste of his own medicine of ease dropping as Jerry was hiding behind the door in the hallway, listening to their entire conversation. Jerry said to himself, "I can't believe that James is in cahoots with this asshole and making plans to kill an unborn child." He started to confront the two men but quickly knew an audience would be required for his point to be heard and their plan would provide the setting. When James returned home that evening, he lied about not having the strength to chat with Roy. When Steph asked "So how'd it go?" He replied "I'm just super pissed right now, I couldn't bring myself to talk about it." "Ok I understand, hey let's just not say anything to anyone until after the class ends." "I think that's a great plan." Later that night, Dave and Steve called him on a three way to check in on how the class was working for him. Steve said, "Wow man, you've been M.I.A since you started. I thought you might have learned a few new tricks and putting two or three kids up in Stephany." James replied "No, not yet but the class is great." Dave said "Yeah I'm glad you decided to go but when are you and Steph going to start having kids?" James sarcastically replied, "Well I think we should see if there is still going to be a marriage first." Dave agreed, "Yeah man, I can only imagine how weird it feels being in there with that guy but it's for the good. And think about it this way, if you and Steph decide to have children, you can thank Roy for helping you make your kid." They all laughed but James couldn't wait to hang up the phone which they all did when Steve said, "Oh I'm getting a cat call from the wife. Good night fellas." Steph also received a three-way call from the girls wanting to know if there was any significant change since James began taking the class. Steph replied, "O yeah, there has certainly been some new developments since he's been taking the class." Both women replied with joys of laughter and congratulating her on a job well done.

CHAPTER 15

Timing

THE DAY HAD finally arrived for James to set up Stephany and he decided to take her to the Reading Terminal Farmers Market. The famous indoors farmer's market had been offering a wide variety of housewares and area specialties for the past century. It was a perfect spot for Stephany to do some shopping and to get some great food. James and Roy decided to meet at 3pm that Saturday, as Jerry was also checking his watch and had plenty of time as it was only 10am in the morning. Jerry went for a quick jog then returned home to continue his plan of destruction. Janet and Marcy was already out in the city doing a little shopping. Dave and his wife rose that morning with intentions of doing a little splurging in the city but was unclear of where they wanted to go. Steve and his family had just left the house in route to the gallery to spoil their little one. Early in the afternoon Mr. and Mrs. Williams went into the city to do a little shopping and purchase some organic foods. Mrs. Williams always wanted to try a more natural way of dieting so this would be a great start. James's parents had just awakened, immediately had gotten dressed and headed into the city to do a little exploring. Dr. Simmons made a few stops in the city during her late afternoon jog. Dr. Clark had a weekend tradition to always stroll through the Reading Terminal and did so that same day. A few hours have passed and everyone has gotten a lot accomplished but still out and about. It's almost 3pm and James mentions that he's hungry and wants to relax. "I'm getting old and I need to sit down." He then chose a nice eatery for them to take a break. After confirming their exact location with a text message, Roy spotted them from a nearby flower shop. But Roy was also seen by Jerry from a nearby Art stand. Stephany saw and waved to her parents who stood in line waiting to get something to eat, Janet and Marcy was also at the market but hadn't seen anything they'd like but also spotted Stephany and James. James's parents also texted their son and told James that they were in the area and spotted each other shortly. Dave's wife Veronica suggested for them to stop by the market and bumped into Steve's wife Carey. Dr. Simmons stopped by the farmer's market to pick up a few items and Dr. Clark toured the area as if he was a complete stranger.

James and Roy made eye contact and when Stephany began eating her sandwich, James excused himself to the bathroom. Seconds later, Roy sat down and wasted no time which Stephany was instantly shocked. "Now you listen to me, I told you from the very beginning that I didn't want any drama and that your husband should go and seek help elsewhere. I did you a favor to help save your marriage and now I need you to do me a favor and get an abortion because this could be bad for my business if the word gets out that I got another man's wife pregnant." He continued demanding for her to get an abortion and not to show her face around the city again.

Strangely, no one saw Roy sitting there chatting with her. The place was completely crowded with folks concentrating on purchasing their items. Stephany replied, "My husband will be returning, you better get lost. Look I know that I put you in a predicament but I'm not sure that I can do that." Before he could respond, Jerry confronted them and kicked over the table and began yelling, "You're a disgusting filthy animal. Everyone, this man who calls himself the whipper has gotten another man's wife pregnant and is here trying to convince her to get an abortion so that his career won't be ruined. He is an absolute fraud who hurts families and is a complete disgrace." Jerry then urged for Roy to get away from Stephany. The customers were frightened by the outburst which several had already began recording the incident on their cellphones. Stephany's parents saw what happened but pretended not to know her. Dave and Steve saw what happened but just stood helplessly. James's parents were baffled and tried to get James on the phone but he didn't answer. Dr. Simmons kept her distance smiling from ear to ear while not noticing that her hair was being sniffed by a horny teenager. Ha-ha! Dr. Clark observed what had taken place and uttered to himself, "Interesting, very interesting."

When Marcy saw Jerry for the first time since they had gotten a divorce, she quickly informed Janet of who he was. "See, I told you he was an asshole, call the cops," and Janet did just that. Others stood by and whispered amongst each other. "Hey, yeah that's the sex instructor guy," "Oh my that's terrible," one elder woman stated. One jokester

shouted, "That's The Whipper? Looks like someone whipped his face."
Hahaha but Stephany just sat there completely exposed and humiliated.
When James returned from hiding in the bathroom his friends and
parents rushed for answers but he was more concerned about his wife.
Jerry continued shouting that both James and Roy were in cahoots but
the police finally arrived and restrained him as he continued to yell
"Prolife, Prolife, adultery is not worse than murder." Marcy then lied to
the police and told them that Jerry was stalking her as he sat handcuffed
in the back of the squad car. After the police confirmed that there
was a restraining order, Jerry was taken in for destruction of property
because he kicked over the table and violating his restraining order. Roy
was totally embarrassed as James ushered Stephany out of the farmer's
market ignoring chants of "Baby Killer, Baby Killer," from those who
were convinced about Jerry's outburst. Both James and Stephany's phone
was lighting up with calls from their friends and family wanting to
know, "What the hell is going on?" But they both agreed not to answer
until they were safe at home. Someone had posted the incident on
YouTube and by the time they reached home, there were death threats
and a few pieces of hate mail in their doorway. James tried to remain
calm and be more concerned about Stephany but once they got settled,
Jerry's tirade seemed to have substance. James's pacing around the house
was suspicious but more so when he asked, "I wonder if Roy will still
be doing the classes?" Instead of asking, "What the hell was Roy doing
sitting there with her in the first place?" Steph remembered that Jerry
was a classmate and when he was shouting about both men being in
cahoots, something just didn't feel right. When James went to bed she
finally decided to answer Janet's call, "Hey Janet, I'm so ashamed but I
really think something fishy is going on." "You know what, Marcy and
I was saying the same thing. How did Roy bravely sit in James's seat and
tell you to get an abortion? The only person that could have told him
that was James. But what did you say to Roy when he first sat down?"
"I told him to leave and that I understand that I placed him in a jam
but an abortion was out of the question." Janet replied, "It all terribly
makes sense that James and Roy was in cahoots like Jerry shouted,
because who else could have taken that kind of information to the sex
classes?" "Yeah Janet you're absolutely right. But I know Marcy feels bad
about lying to the police that Jerry was stalking her." "Yes, she does so
she already decided not to show up at court so they'll eventually drop

the violation charge but he'll still have to deal with the others charges for vandalizing the store. This is certainly an interesting turn of events because first you kept Roy a secret, then you managed to have both men working together, now they're trying to keep secrets from you." LOL! The two ladies shared a laugh before hanging up and Stephany went to confront James who was also on the phone chatting with his dad. "Look son today was a bad day, and your mother and I are really concerned about you. I mean how many guys would have been able to see the bigger picture, lower their ego and get sex lessons from his wife's lover? That's really something special but maybe it's time to consider getting a divorce son. This woman is bringing you too much drama and taking advantage of your kind heart, and its killing your mother and I who just have to sit back and watch." James replied, "You know what Pop, if I said that the thought of a divorce never crossed my mind, I would be lying, but the fact is, I started something and I would like to finish it. Minus the mishap today, the classes are helping me and since it's my marriage, I would like for you and mom to continue giving me your most generous support whether or not I decide to continue with this union."

"Well said son, your mother and I will continue to do so." Stephany then entered the room just as James hung up the phone and asked, "So who was that?" "That was your loyal Father in-law assuring us that we had his most generous support and to stay strong." "Really? Well maybe that was a lesson you missed about generous support." "James looked confused but knew she was on to something. Steph asked, "Did you tell your father about the little roll you played in trying to set me up with Roy?" She then became sarcastic, "You would think that you would be the last person to try and set me up with Roy." "Ok enough, yes Roy and I came up with a plan where he would try and talk you out of having the baby." "Unbelievable, two headed monsters. Not that it was going to work, but I guess Jerry was the savior of the day." James apologized then turned on the Ten o'clock news where he and Stephany both watched protesters provide Roy with a few choice words and threatened to Boycott his sex class. James and Steph were in disbelief but more so, the very next day when hundreds of people signed a petition to have the class discontinued. When Dave and Steve finally got a hold of James, James simply explained that it was a last minute plan that obviously went horribly wrong. Steve joked, "Wow, you guys really hit it off. Now you're making plans with this guy." Dave really felt bad for James but was also concerned about the other students who was affected by his stupidity. Social media had a field day with Roy and he eventually had to shut down the class prematurely. But premature wasn't a good term for Stephany's condition, so James accompanied her to a Doctor's appointment in the early morning to make sure all was well as she remained in the early stages of her pregnancy. Stephany also continued to tease James about his so called master plan. "So Roy isn't going to suddenly appear trying to give me the examination is he?" James fired back "You know, that actually isn't a bad idea. I should have asked him to come along so just in case the baby belongs to him, you guys won't miss out on early bonding." "You're an asshole." Her name was then called by the doctor who confirmed that a little bleeding in the vaginal area could seem scary for a first time mother but all was well. Before heading home, they stopped and grabbed some lunch. As they sat in the gallery food court, Stephany was repeatedly congratulated on her gestation and that made James totally disregard if the child was not of his bloodline. He was accustomed to receiving attention and people raving about his accomplishments and hard work but this kind of devotion was oddly more satisfying. And rightfully so, he had created a multi-million-dollar establishment and managed employees but there was a sense of urgency which he was willing to accept. This was a feeling of uncertainty, failures, laughter, sensitivity, love, frustration and most importantly patience. He loved it and James wasn't going to rob himself of experiencing the next phase of accomplishing greatness. After chowing down on his delicious chicken wrap sandwich from chipotle, James envisioned picking his child up from basketball or football practice, wearing matching preppy outfits with his son or being nagged by his daughter about wanting a new sun dress.

He saw what appeared to be a single father just having lunch with his children by a well-designed water fountain. The sight of another younger family was basically a preview of what he and Stephany could expect. The younger couple's public display of affection might have been overly exhibited but it was exciting to see true love blossoming. But James never shared his thoughts with Stephany, he just continued to observe his surroundings like a territorial cat as Stephany had a few thoughts of her own. She immediately thought about whether her or James would be giving the sex talk, which school would be the best option because home schooling was certainly not an option. She really didn't care about the sex of the baby as long as the child was healthy. But when they strolled passed a kids clothing store, James accidentally thought out loud, "My son will certainly be a clothes horse." Steph gave him a shocking look and said "Yes James if it's a boy, he will certainly have your mannerism of being well dressed. She also expressed her preference to have a boy. "Boys are so much easier to manipulate when they're kids and less expensive to shop for. Girls have more variety to choose, and you have to be more sensitive with them. Right now I'm the only woman in the house and I'm not ready to share my emotional crown just yet. Girls certainly require more attention than boys and I can't handle a two-year-old being impatient." James replied, "Well it's going to be a learning process for both of us and I'm looking forward to the on the job training." Steph then said, "Our parents are going to spoil this child rotten but I know Marcy or Janet would be worse, if either were chosen to be the God Mother." "I can't believe I'm saying this but since Janet was your maid of honor, Marcy should be the God Mother." "Wow, well I'm not really surprised. Marcy would make an excellent God mother. I'm sure that she would be honored and wouldn't care what the sex is, as long as it's a healthy baby. But if there's something wrong with the child then Marcy wouldn't want any parts." LOL!

Their nice relaxing outing turned solemn when James mentioned, "Hey to be honest, if that's the way she really felt, and you're not just trying to be funny, I would agree with her." Steph replied, "You know what, I don't even want to think about if something was to go wrong. But you wouldn't want to keep the baby if the doctors said something went wrong?" "Absolutely not, I don't have time for that, nor do I want to complicate our life style. God forbid the doctors did say that something is going wrong with OUR CHILD, the best thing to do is have a procedure done to terminate the pregnancy. I only want to help with the diaper changing for the first two years, not twenty-five years." "Well when you put it like that, I'm certainly on board to terminate the pregnancy, only if the doctor said that something was going wrong." Steph ordered a fruit salad and they continued to admire the little children who were either misbehaving or safely glued to their parent's side. As they continued to stroll, Steph began looking a little worried until James brightened the mood. "But I'm certainly confident that all will be well. A matter of fact I'm so confident that I think we should go and purchase a baby crib while we're here. We'll have it delivered and when it arrives, me and the fellas will put it together. "Aww James that's so sweet. Ok let's go." They went to Babies "R" us and purchased a white Sorelle Princeton 4-in-1 Convertible Crib & Changer for four hundred bucks. James thought about hauling it to the car but was too lazy and just stuck with the original plan of having it delivered. What a way to put Stephany back in good spirits and assuring that he would be there 110%. James had basically declared himself to be the modern day Joseph, who was the earthly father of Jesus.

CHAPTER 16

New Pain

THE CRIB ARRIVED a few days later. Instead of waiting for James to come home with Dave and Steve, Steph decided to begin putting the crib together herself. She did a horrible job. When the guys got home they discreetly made fun of her attempt while placing the pieces correctly. Dave teased, "Poor Steph she began placing the safety bars on the changing table instead of the crib." LOL! Although she was down stairs sorting out laundry, Steph could hear them questioning James about who would be the better God father?" She smiled when hearing James struggle to answer because of the surprising question and having to suddenly choose between two of his only true friends. He playfully responded, "Neither of you, you both suck," then quickly walked out of the room. Steve whispered to Dave, "Man, this is almost like the story of Jesus" Dave asked "How so?" "Remember in the story where Mary tells her husband Joseph that she is pregnant by God and at first Joseph gets pissed but eventually buys into what she said and then they set out to have a happy family?" "Oh yeah, that's true. But I sure hope that the baby belongs to James. He's such a great guy and deserves to be happy." About twenty minutes later, James returned and the crib was complete. The entire nursery was complete because the walls were already painted a nice sun yellow unisex color. The proud parents to be were thrilled at the job they had done. When James offered them one hundred dollars each, they rejected the money with Steve mentioning, "Oh no buddy you're trying to get off cheap. I smell food. What is Stephany cooking? "Hahaha, James answered "We're having turkey chops with brown rice and vegetables." Steve replied "Ok cool, I'll have a large portion of that instead." James smiled while replying, "No problem." But Dave said, "Well, I'll also have some food and his share of the money." LOL! All was granted and dinner was delicious. After dinner, the guys played a few rounds of pool in the man cave. Both guys congratulated him on having such nobility and assured James that they were in his corner. He thanked them both, right before he scratched on the six ball and lost the game against Dave.

Steve was aware of the possible awkwardness but still asked James, "Hey so do you feel like you learned something from the sex class?" Dave stopped counting his money and fiercely anticipated a response. "You know I actually did. It was really great for my self-esteem. Although I can't really apply all of the techniques that I learned because her stomach is getting so big, but it makes me very excited to see what the future has to offer." Dave expressed his sympathy. "And you were so close to completing the class." James replied, "Yeah but its ok. I sure hope all is well with Roy, it's kind of crazy the way things ended but I sure hope he lands on his feet." Steve agreed, "Yes I'm not really surprised that you would show some sort of genuine concern for him. Come to think of it, he not only helped to better our marriages he strengthened our friendships towards each other as well." Dave thought Steve was just being overly sensitive or just blowing smoke and tested him. "How did Roy better our friendship?" Steve answered "Well maybe I should have spoken for myself, but Roy helped me to also be able to trust again because no one else knows that I was having trouble in the bedroom. You guys are the only ones besides my wife of course, and I trust that you both would keep it to yourselves." James agreed with Steve. "Yes that's true. I certainly had trust issues before I took the class. I'm honestly not 100% there with you two yet, but I'm certainly working hard to getting there, that's why you're both here tonight to build these memories with me and Stephany. I want us to be friends. Both men smiled and agreed. James was being truthful about wanting to be friends but up until this moment he was not being honest with himself because he was happy that the class had ended prematurely because his temper was about to explode. So although James admitted that he did learn something from the class, during this time the last person he wanted to discuss was Roy. But a deep concern fell upon Dave and Steve because they were doing well and Roy was left disgraced and ruined.

"We need to do something" Dave said. James annoyingly asked "Ok, I took the class, so what else am I supposed to do now?" Dave answered "Real talk, you took that class because your wife demanded for you to take it, so how can you get upset if I, as your trustworthy friend is recommending for you to help this man that more than likely now needs your help?" James was stubborn, "You're acting like he did me a favor and I took the class for free." Steve chimed in, "Wow if he offered it to you for free that would have really been bad. Hahaha." James continued, "Furthermore, did everyone here forget that I might be taking care of this guy's kid?" Dave replied, "Man you're confused and not being honest with yourself. You can't keep saying Oh this guy's kid and throwing that in people's faces, it's your kid to, you have to take the entire package deal if you're going to stay with Stephany, not just take care of the child when it's convenient for you." "Good point." Steph cheered while wobbling down the steps because she overheard them on the baby walkie, that she bought and placed one in the man cave but the guys never noticed it. She actually bought one for every room in the house. She then showed them the walkie talky, thanked both men for their time, then showed them the door. She then scolded James. "I'm not going to play cat and mouse with you or continue on this roller coaster ride. I'd rather pack my stuff now and save us all the drama." James admitted "Yes you're right, I have to work on that. It's basically a contradiction of sincerely forgiving. But this Roy chapter is over. Just like I mentioned to the guys, I'm not 100% healed yet but I'm trying. I'm trying with everyone, that's why we're all here. It was a learning experience and I would like to move on with you."

Months later, the baby was due any day now. Although James told Steph and the guys that it really didn't matter if the baby was his biological child, he secretly kept his curiosity just to maintain a peaceful home. James had no intentions of playing the fool, so on that rainy morning of April 1st, 2015 at 6:35 am when baby Zena was born, James refused to sign the papers and firmly asked for a paternity test. "The white mid age male doctor who delivered the baby was stern as well. "That request is normal; it might be unsettling for the mother but the law says she has the right to choose, so you should have the right to know whether this child is yours or not. We will have those results for you in one week Mr. Pain." When the nurse held the baby like a dirty diaper when giving her to James, he almost flung the new born across the room. The baby was ugly and looked exactly like Roy. The nursing staff quickly exited the room so that the new parents could have some quality time. If it was up to James, the child would have been discarded and would never have seen the light of day. Stephany just laid there completely exhausted from the useless epidural and could care less who the baby belonged to. LOL! She was just happy to end the relentless labor pains. When the guys got to the hospital, Dave's face turned more pale than Steve's face. They both looked at James as if to say, "Well what are you going to do?" James just said I'll get the test results in one week. When her parents got there her mother immediately said a "Hail Mary." They looked at James and he repeated, "I get the test results in one week." "When his parents got there, they both grimaced but offered the highest common sanction. "God bless all three of you." "James repeated, "I get the test results in one week." His father's chuckling was a representation of asking, "What more proof would you need?" When Janet and Marcy reached the hospital, Marcy was certainly beside herself with excitement. When Marcy laid eyes on the baby then looked around at the faces of everyone else, the entire six floor could hear her laughing but Janet was nice enough to take pictures. Before James could say the words, everyone in the room shouted, "HE GETS THE TEST RESULTS IN ONE WEEK." LOL! When they took home the four pound three ounce new born, some of the neighbors sneered at the child like an awful stench whenever Stephany removed her covers. The next few days would be painful. James's intentions were great and he thought that he could hang in there. His friends and family provided their most generous support as promised but when reality touched down, James found himself looking in the apartment guide checking for a new bachelor's pad. He realized that Stephany was right, it was better to allow her to pack her stuff and just leave rather than continue on this emotional roller coaster and constantly being indecisive. Two days before he got the test results he remembered Dave mentioning something about helping Roy. While staring at the baby, James thought about helping Roy to an early grave. But James wasn't completely a jerk that week. He did the minor things. He helped with the feeding and clothing then handed the baby back to her mother when she needed changing. Come to think of it, that's exactly what the average new father does. LOL! When the big day arrived, the tension arose early that morning before the sun greeted the rocky couple. James just laid in bed staring at the wall and thinking to himself that it was a complete waste of time trying to find answers he already knew. The last week felt like an eternity but it wouldn't take long for Stephany to sign the divorce papers once paternity was established.

Their appointment at the hospital was scheduled for 9am. James's plan was simple. "Don't even return back to the home with Stephany.

He even packed a suit case that morning and reserved a hotel until he found another place to live. He was well rested and eager, while a hellishly fatigued Stephany struggled with her new mommy duties during the night. James thought he'd fully disposed of the apartment guides but as he and Stephany sat in the bumper to bumper morning traffic, she blurted, "I noticed a few apartment guides in the trashcan and saw the ones that you circled. You have horrible taste." He replied, "Yes obviously I have terrible taste. I will be sure to work on that." Stephany then turns vicious, "I guess you can just send my belongings to my parent's house until I get an apartment." He's twice as brutal, "Well I sure hope they've been looking in the apartment guide because they better find somewhere else to live." She now wants to stab James and rip his eye balls out of socket but there's nothing in sight to commit the evil deed. She's seconds away from getting out of the car and taking the bus but the public transportation in the suburban area sucked. James continued to run his mouth. Her conscience was telling her not to say another word or she'll insanely begin using the baby as a weapon to issue the beating. They could have saved themselves a trip by having the documents emailed or texted to either of their cellphones but James preferred his pending embarrassment to be revealed the old fashion way. They arrive on time but the staff is just arriving as well. The nurses, the technicians and transporters were calm, cool, and collected but could probably feel the raging heat between Stephany and James while on the elevator. A security guard informed them of the correct room which they sat next to each other and waited patiently along with two other couples. The mothers were looking completely furious and Stephany offered one of them some tissue as the ESPN high lights seemed to momentarily distract the guy's fury. The doctor finally entered the room and called in one of the couples. Minutes later everyone on the floor could hear the supposed to be father celebrating and insulting the woman because the test results proved that he was not the biological father.

"Ha Ha Ha. The guy then began throwing job applications from a local strip club at the woman and demanding for her to go find a damn job and stop looking for handouts. The remaining couples were amused but the staff continued to work because more than likely they were accustomed to seeing that type of reaction on a daily basis. The doctor returned and called in the other couple. The result was the same which proved that the guy was not the father but he quietly left the building.

The doctor asked the young woman were there any more candidates that she could think of because he was the eighth guy that month to pass the test. He then gave her sometime to think about it and returned to the waiting room and called Stephany and James. The doctor was a bit unprofessional by mentioning, "This is a rare case, I don't recall in my ten years doing a paternity test for a married couple, well better safe than sorry." Neither of them gave a response and just sat there awaiting their fate. There were several other envelopes and the doctor checked to make sure that he had the correct one before stating, "Zena Pain was born on April 1st, 2015 at 6:35 am. The paternity test results show that Mr. James Pain is 99.9 % the biological father of the child. Congratulations sir." "What? What the hell? Are you serious?" James surprisingly asked. The doctor showed them both the test results and said that he would be glad to make them a copy for their own personal records. The doctor further explained. To be honest, I think all new borns are ugly. But a child really doesn't begin to develop a parents features until after the first couple of years." "Yes, thank you Doctor," James replied. Before the doctor left the office he asked, "Are you three going to be alright, as you can see we don't need any more drama around here this morning." James assured the good doctor that all was well but when the doctor left the office seconds later, there were loud screams that frightened everyone. Surprisingly, James began rejoicing and shouting, "Thank God for DNA, it just proved that I'm the father of this beautiful baby girl." He received a brief round of applause from the entire floor then apologized to Stephany. She also extended her own regret for contributing to this maddening confusion. They left the building but not before leaving a few nurses teary eyed.

How Ironic that James never wanted his family and friends to be in his business but they were the first ones he called once he received the great news. His parents of course were shocked but were glad that their prayers had come through. His mother immediately made plans for her granddaughters first birthday party, prom, and her wedding day. LOL! James's father sarcastically but seriously asked "Are you sure? Take it again." Marcy and Janet were thrilled and instantly made plans to see the baby. After the relieving conclusion it made sense for the Pain family to invite everyone to their home for a get together. James still didn't care too much for her friends but it was a celebration and everyone was invited. The gifts for baby Zena were in abundance but Marcy was more interested in the multiple options of adult beverages. Her mother was a great co-host and prowled the room making sure everyone was having a great time. The party felt like a mixture of a baby shower and a Christmas bash but a moment of gravity was at helm when James made a touching speech. "I would like to thank everyone for coming but more so for your support throughout our ups and downs. You guys could have been doing anything else in the world with your time but you chose to entertain our dilemmas and I thank you for providing the fuel to make me continue to prove my undying love for this beautiful woman. I am a happy man that's certainly looking forward to the future with my beautiful family." Steph added a few words after breast feeding and Janet adored little Zena while checking her phone three times to make sure the pictures were saved. It was a great day in the Pain house hold. The air was finally cleared in regards to the paternity test and what a relief. But something was still riding heavy on James's conscience. One afternoon while Roy sat outside with his janitor colleagues having lunch, the BMW i8 pulled in front of his job. He immediately thought that it was Stephany but it was James that stepped out of the vehicle. James had gone back to the dealership and was lucky enough to get the car back. Everyone thought there was going to be an altercation between the two men but James greeted Roy with a smile and reached in his pocket and pulled out a check for Fifty Thousand dollars and gave it to Roy. James whispered, "I just wanted to say thank you, you helped me and my family." In addition to the fifty grand, James gave Roy some hotel vouchers so he could fly around the country hosting seminars teaching men how to have better sex. The grudge was finally buried and he felt at piece. There was no announcement that was made about how kind he was to Roy, because before James departed their embrace spoke volumes.

CHAPTER 17

Vacation

NOW THAT THE mentally disturbing roller coaster had finally ended, it was perfect timing for a vacation. James first considered that maybe it should just be for him and Stephany. When Steph asked her mother about babysitting, Mrs. Williams sure didn't mind. "Most certainly, it would be just like old times when I use to feed and check up on you in the middle of the night." But her father thought otherwise. "So that means our hanky panky night will be interrupted, just like old times. Nice." Steph was happy to have the support but her separation anxiety kicked in, so baby Zena would be going along to the magnificent one-week trip to their pending destination. Steph was concerned about getting sea sick, so the option of a cruise was eliminated. James didn't like the idea of flying because of his ears being painfully clogged when going through the air pack. After receiving a great all-inclusive package deal for the Half Moon resort area in Montego Bay Jamaica, they booked the first flight and boarded the one hundred fifty passenger bird early that morning. It was a straight flight to the beautiful paradise and they were exhausted when reaching the hotel. But the staff was extremely friendly and Ms. Clarisse an older staff member even held baby Zena and was able to stop her from crying as James and Steph gathered their belongings. Their suite was fantastic. It featured a pool front view, shaded by mango trees. The atmosphere was breathtaking but James was more fascinated because he had never heard or seen a white woman with a Jamaican accent. The woman had gray eyes and blonde Dred Locks. Stephany was inside tending to the child while he relaxed outside. He notices the woman sitting by the pool along with her two dark complexioned friends. They're laughing and playfully caressing each other. The woman appears to be in her late twenties and is exceptionally appealing. James continued to stare until he and the beautiful woman made eye contact. She can tell that he is a foreigner and waved to say hello. The lovely trio continued laughing and began smoking marijuana.

One of the girls whispered something in the white woman's ear then all three of them began making their way towards James. His smile was getting bigger as they were now only a few feet away from him. Then Stephany came outside looking terrible and gave him the baby. It was an absolute spoiler as the lovely ladies instantly turned around and walked away. LOL! But the beautiful woman turned her head and admired James holding his daughter. Steph and James decided to stay in that night. As she slept, James saw another older white married couple by the pool. They were having a great time as the woman was sitting on her husband's lap laughing at his jokes. It was a reminder for James that, the real reason he was here was to spend quality time with his family, not stare down and lust after exotic ass. They woke the next morning and decided to have breakfast at the beach restaurant. They're greeted by an older male waiter with a heavy accent who assures them they'll enjoy the fresh taste of the ackee and salt fish with fried dumplings. They accepted the recommendation from the enthusiastic waiter with Stephany attempting to add one order of rum punch but is having trouble finding her I.D. The waiter informed her to "Please take your time," then walked away. She continued to dig in her purse while James was holding baby Zena. The beautiful woman from the pool then strolled by and waved at James as he foolishly waved back. Stephany looked up just in time to catch him and asked, "Who were you waving to?" He nervously but honestly replied, "I don't know, that woman just walked by and waved to me, maybe she thinks I'm a famous basketball player."

"Yeah real funny." The food arrived and they inhaled the meal then headed to the beach for a little relaxation. During this time, the beautiful woman was by herself standing knee deep in the ocean, taking in the elements. She isn't paying them any attention but Stephany felt the need to point her out to James.

"There goes your little girl friend, she looks lonely." James didn't notice her but it was perfect timing as the beautiful woman began taking out her wedgie and Stephany tried to cover his eyes. Stephany is obviously intimidated but James reassures her that, "You're my girlfriend, my wife and my best friend," then seals the sentimental statement with a kiss that is now seen by the beautiful woman. The sun begins to rage and they returned to the hotel. It was nap time for the baby, so Steph stayed inside while James relaxed under a tree near the pool. Shortly after getting comfortable he's joined by the older married couple he saw the first night laughing and joking. They introduced themselves and began a very interesting conversation. Bill and Rose were from Manhattan, New York. The real estate power couple owned a few condos in the big apple and was visiting their niece that lived in Jamaica. Of course they were impressed with James. Rose was very flirtatious and almost sitting on James's lap while laughing at his jokes. They never asked James was he married or had children but Rose thought it would be a great idea for him to meet their niece. Rose then went inside leaving the two men to continue chatting about sports and their next vacation destination. When Rose returned she said, "James I would like for you to meet my niece this is, Geneva." Wow, what a coincidence. It's the beautiful woman that has been flirting with him from a far. James is overwhelmed by his nerves and dropped his drink when shaking her hand. She's well-tanned and ferociously amazing up-close.

Rose continued, "Yes she tends to have that effect on men. She's certainly cut from a different type of cloth." Geneva responds in her sexy accent "Ok auntie I'm standing right here. It was nice meeting you James." James is completely paranoid and knows that he should get his ass away from these people. Steph could come outside any minute and rightfully rip him to shreds. He made an attempt to leave until Rose shoved some more drinks down his throat and said "Come on Bill, it's our hanky panky time, leave the kids alone." This was bad, but James had a few extra minutes to spare because Steph sent a text message saying she would also be taking a nap. Geneva was soft spoken when asking, "So are you having a great time?" The alcohol did in fact help him to relax. "Yes I'm having a wonderful time, NOW." She laughed then became very curious about his profession. "Are you a basketball player?" "Hahaha, no I sell apartments, similar to your uncle, here is a picture of my building." She laughed and replied yes selling apartments that's his side job for a supplemental income. He really sells Villas, like the one you and your wife is staying in, my uncle is part owner of this entire resort." James felt like small potatoes. "Sorry, did I to make you feel like small potatoes?" "No, no not at all," and took another sip of his drink as she continued. "The one thing my uncle taught me was, it's about being able to live the same or a better lifestyle than the so called idols while having a completely different profession." James agreed, "Yes that's true because there are more people in the world that can read and write, than can run and jump." When she smiled at his logic, he almost dropped the drink again. The environment was serene; they were in heaven so she had absolutely no intentions of coming to America. When she rubbed his wavy hair, his concealed erection instantly became visible. "Awww... that's cute you're attracted to me. So what are you going to do about it?" Stephany was sure to be sleeping for at least another hour and Geneva's place was a few feet away, so James jumped up and said, "Let's go OUR SEPARATE WAYS. It was nice meeting you Geneva." He was in a different country and amazed at the beautiful easy women. But it certainly wasn't worth losing his family over a moment of bliss. The next morning James is in bed sleeping, but Stephany awoke early. She's in the mood to go for a walk on the beach but first makes a bottle for baby Zena and puts it in the fridge. She then leaves a note for James explaining her ware bouts. It's a beautiful cool morning. Other tourist and locals are strolling alongside the gorgeous sand beach. There is a notoriously arrogant, Jamaican track star whose sprints were interrupted by some on lookers for autographs but he's humbled enough to bless the few fans with his penmanship. He noticed Stephany not joining the handful of harassers and felt the need to inquire, "Oh so you don't like me?" She's just as aggressive, "Excuse me but I don't even know you." "Oh, ok sorry." She can tell that his feelings were hurt but serves him right for not properly introducing himself but he eventually does so. "My name is Blizz, I'm the star for Jamaica's track team." Stephany almost melted and instantly became apologetic. "Oh my God, Blizz yes I'm so sorry. I usually just see you on television. Yes, I'm here in Jamaica so I guess it makes sense why I would run into you here." "Hahaha, yes you're in Jamaica," he said while smiling revealing that electrifying smile. He continued and asked "So what is your name?" Now she should have said I'm a married woman nice meeting you and continued on her way but she replied, "My name is Stephany." "Well Ms. Stephany it was nice meeting you. I would love to stay and chat but I have some running to do." "Well, would you like me to join you or would I be too much of a distraction?" This bitch is crazy and asking for trouble. Blizz laughed and replied, "Sure you can join me; a little motivation won't hurt." But Stephany was a distraction. The only running that took place was their mouths and Stephany forgetting that she was on vacation with her HUSBAND. They continued to stroll the beach as she finally decided to mention, "I just got married and had a baby so I need to get back in shape." "Wow, you just had a baby, your body is unbelievable." She's smiling ridiculously because James never told her that after she gave birth. When she showed Blizz her ugly stretch marks, he replied, "Ok, you earned your stripes, so those marks mean that you're a tiger now."

She continued blushing and when the breeze blew he gently removed her hair from her face. "Thank you." "You're welcome beautiful. Hey I'm staying at the "Secret Wild Orchid" hotel, it's right over there. She's amazed by the spectacular scenery. He continued, "I've been doing extremely well and my peoples are throwing me a surprise party, so I have to pretend not to know what's going on. But I would love for you to come, bring your husband so we all can celebrate." "Well that sounds like fun, Ok I'll be there." "Great, come on I'll race you back to your place." They returned within minutes and Blizz simply waved goodbye. She anticipated James still sleeping, the baby needing to be fed and changed. But when she entered James was up feeding the baby. He had also prepared a nice morning breakfast for her while she was out dallying with the handsome star. "Wow, this looks delicious." James made some fried plantains, eggs and toasted bread. He replied "Yes, it's delicious but you sure look edible." "Why thank you my handsome King." "So what's the plan for today?" "Oh some folks are throwing a surprise party for Blizz, the Jamaican track star and we got invited. It's not until later tonight so we can just relax and go later." "So, you want to take a new born baby to a party with a bunch of loud drunk strangers?" "Yeah it will be fun. We can take turns holding her and touring the Wild Secret Orchid." "Oh that place is wonderful. It's just on the other side of the beach. Ok I guess we can take Zena to her first party." As the morning continued to blossom, James snapped a few photos of the beautiful sunrise, while Stephany struggled to choose one of her sexy bikinis for the party. "Hey Sweetie which one should I wear?" "Hmm... wear the turquoise one. But make sure it has a cover, I'm not in the mood to get into a fist fight with one of these young thunder cats." Although Blizz made her feel extra special about her stretch marks, she had every intentions of sporting a cover over the bikini.

Later than evening they got dressed and were one of the first guest to arrive early at the party. Folks eventually started pouring in but Blizz still hadn't made his surprised entrance. It was a very diverse atmosphere and all were having a great time drinking and enjoying the dance hall music. "SURPRISE," and Blizz finally appeared looking relaxed in his green trunks and white Jamaican t-shirt. He signed dozens of autographs, pulled out his selfie stick and took about a hundred photos. He did a great job on pretending to be surprised but was truly excited that Stephany was able to make it. He spotted her being hit on by some much younger guys. "Hey, you came, I'm so surprised. "I really didn't think you were going to make it," He said. "Lucky for you I didn't have anything else to do. Nice place." "Thank you, Thank you. So where is your husband?" He's standing over there, surrounded by your cheerleaders." "Hahaha, I see but before I came over, you had quite an entourage yourself." "Yeah right, I quickly informed those barely legal guys that I was not a cougar and to run along." "Yes you're far too young to be a cougar." She then momentarily left to check on James. He was having a great time sucking up all the attention that baby Zena was bringing but the young ladies quickly disbursed once momma bear approached. James assured, "I'm having a great time bonding with my daughter please don't interrupt." LOL! The DJ gave Blizz a huge shout out and the crowd went wild. Stephany's cellphone rang but it was just her mother checking up to see if all was well. By the time Steph returned back to see Blizz, he was completely surrounded by a group of supermodels. She briefly stood by herself but didn't know that Blizz's bedroom door was right behind her. Seconds later, the door opened and Blizz snatched her into the dark elegantly stunning room with a gorgeous ocean view. He threw her on the bed as she wrapped her arms around him. Surprisingly, the bed never caught on fire because of their flaming kiss. Blizz was the track star but Stephany couldn't have gotten up and ran out of there any faster. "No, I can't do this. I'M MARRIED."

She went to the bathroom to wash her face and grabbed her husband then went home. During the entire walk home, James was jabbering about how much of a great time baby Zena was having. Steph said, "Yeah, you mean the great time that you were having using our baby as a chick magnet." "So did you have a great time sweetie?" She paused then looked at James and answered, "Yeah it was very interesting. Great atmosphere and some really fun people." "We kind of left just in time because I started to smell marijuana." James might have smelled marijuana but it was Stephany that was coming down from her high. The following day they just relaxed as a family, took a bunch of photos and assisted others with capturing some memorable moments. The day before their last on the island, they laid in bed and congratulated each other on sticking with their marriage. James suggested that, it would be a perfect time to renew their vows. One of the couples that they helped take a few pictures was a Pastor and his wife from New Orleans. Both had deep southern accents. James and Steph first explained the issues they were having in their marriage to Pastor Fisher. James apologized for possibly inconveniencing the couple who were celebrating their 25th Anniversary but explained, "We just don't want to return home as the same lustful couple. This vacation was fun but substance is necessary. I want God to bless our marriage so that I can be able to enjoy and please my beautiful wife." The Pastor was sorry to hear about the early tribulations but was overjoyed to facilitate the private ceremony which took place the next morning. They began their new path to a better marriage dressed in matching lime green and white colors and renewed their vows on the beach with some on lookers that included Geneva and Blizz.

CHAPTER 18

Prayed

WHEN THEY RETURNED home and got settled, before bed, James opened the Bible and read the story of Abraham's wife Sarah giving birth at age 88. Sarah thought that she could not conceive and prayed about her issue. That's when it dawned on James that he had never prayed about his problems. Instead of praying which James clearly needed a miracle, he and his wife turned to their friends for guidance and other seductive ventures. He then mentioned it just as Steph was finishing up on flossing her teeth. "Here's a thought, why don't we pray about it?" "Sure honey, great idea." "I mean, we dug ourselves a pretty deep whole, I'm thankful for the Reverend but I just think we have some more work to do on our own." "You know what? I totally agree with that and I also have an idea." "What's that babe?" "How about we practice celibacy?" "Celibacy? But we're married." "I know, I rather for us to have bad sex in the beginning of our marriage and figure it out later, then to be one of those couples who sleeps in separate bedrooms or stupidly stay together for the sake of the kids." "I feel you." "So if we're going to start over, lets pray about it and start over the right way." "This actually sounds like a great idea. Since its celibacy, sex is not supposed to be on our minds anyway and we can focus on bettering our marriage in other areas." "Yeah honey, that's right then great sex will come naturally." "But wait a minute" James said, "I thought that I was the man of your dreams and everything was perfect, except for my sex being atrocious, so what other areas do I need to work on?" "Oh honey come on, we can all improve as long as we're alive." "No, no, no, I think you're trying to find something else wrong with me so I can work more than I'm supposed to be doing." "Oh that's insane, ok maybe just a little." "Too bad you can't find anything. Haha"

"I only tried to find something wrong so you could remain perfect in those other areas." "You don't have to try and find anything wrong with me Ms. Crazy, I'm always going to be on point for the both of us. But shall we pray?" "We shall." That night James asked the good Lord to continue blessing their marriage so he could please his wife in other areas and to be strong and wise during their time of celibacy. "Celibacy?" hahahahaa is that your solution Steve asked during guy's night out. "I've never heard of such baloney." "It may be unorthodox but it's going to work for us," James assured. "So you guy's never thought of applying the concept of "Practice makes perfect?" Dave asked. James jokingly replied "Come on man, you're talking about practice, who cares about practice?" Then took a sip of his beer. "Wow man, I guess you guys are really exhausting every option to make sure your marriage works," Steve stated. "Yeah, Stephany is a really special person because truthfully, if the shoe was on the other foot and sex was really important to me, I would have left her ass a long time ago and found happiness elsewhere." "Wow that's deep, but I respect that." Dave said, "But if my wife had that issue I would probably stay and get some good loving on the side. What man seriously wants to live unfulfilled?" "Man I probably would do the same damn thing. Have my cake and eat it to, especially if I knew she was a great girl but her sex was just bad." Steve added. "So how long is this celibacy thing supposed to go on for?" Dave asked. "We really didn't agree on a time frame? But let me send a text and ask." Steph replied by asking how long did he have in mind? He replied until tonight with a happy face. LOL! She replied two months. "Hey she said two months." "That's not too bad, that's about the average time it usually takes a young couple to start having sex anyway, Steve said." "That would be a great question, James thought. "Let me ask someone." There was another trio of beautiful women sitting across from them at the bar. James walked over and asked, "Excuse me ladies, sorry to interrupt, how long does it take for either of you to start having sex with a guy that you're dating?" The first woman said "Maybe a couple of weeks or a month, it depends on the chemistry." The second woman looked at her and called her a whore, then answered usually several months." The last woman said, that she was practicing celibacy but before it was usually around a couple of months." "Wow, Celibacy? So how's that working for you?" James asked. "It's great, of course I have my moments and hot guys like you cause me to almost relapse but so far so good. It's been a year for me." "Thank you so much ladies for entertaining me, I would like buy you each a drink." James bought them each a "Sex on the Beach," then returned to his friends. It was also a lady's night and Steph and the girls were at Marcy's place drinking and having a great time, especially when Steph mentioned "James and I are practicing celibacy." Marcy burst out laughing while holding a bottle of strawberry rum. "It just keeps getting better with you two doesn't it," Marcy jeered. "It's something new, but of course a mutual agreement," Steph defended. "Something new?" Marcy asked, "Let's hear this one." "Well when James and I went to Jamaica, we renewed our vows. So we also decided to start fresh and start over with no sex. We can concentrate on bettering other areas of our marriage."

Janet was impressed. "That's actually pretty good Steph, I'm proud of the both of you. See now you're thinking." Marcy contested, "So, let me get this straight, James has bad sex and he cheated, now he won't be having any sex at all and you don't think he's going to cheat? This should be interesting." Steph replied, "It seems to be working pretty good so far, I haven't been feeling horny?" "Well how long has it been?" Marcy asked. "Just a few days" "Wait until after a couple of weeks you're going to be one hot tamale." "Well that's great because we're actually doing it for two months, since I guess that's the average time couples start having sex anyway." "Your generation moves too fast" Janet affirmed. "Back in my day, it would take two months for a guy to get my phone number. Now you women give up the goodies in two months or less, no wonder the men have such low standards. Sex in two months, that's terrible, nowadays marriages aren't even lasting that long. Whoa how times have changed." To confirm what Janet said was true, Marcy posted a question on Facebook asking "What is your average wait time for sex when meeting someone new?" A few people replied, "Depends on how horny I am and how cute he is." Another stated, sometimes you just have to hurry up and get sex from them before they try and get sex from you," LOL. But several others replied that six months to a year was their standard time frame. Marcy then posted asking the guys "How long did they expect to start having sex when meeting a woman?" And as expected a few jerks said, "That same night. LOL. Some elaborated that anything over a few month was way too long, especially if the woman is already comfortable with inviting you to her house and she's visiting your home, then sex should be involved." James and Stephany worked on their marriage by going clothes shopping together, instead of James just giving her the money and she hitting the mall with her girlfriends.

They exercised together with early morning runs and evening family walks with the baby.

Yes, there were nights when both were tempted so James went back into the guest room to minimize his frustration. Watching Steph in the kitchen was a turn-on but he sharpened her skills by helping her with the cooking. She kept him on a pedal stole where he rightfully belonged. She did her job as a respectable wife and provided genuine compliments over the gold digging gestures from passing waywards. These new substitutes helped introduce them to a different level of support and appreciation for each other. Abstinence during marriage also helped them bill up the fire and excitement about being with each other. It was basically separating themselves physically from each other, all while still remaining married and living under the same roof. To others abstinence during marriage sounded absurd but it reinvented their union. For James, the fresh start felt like the beginning of the third quarter after having a terrible first half in a basketball game. Stephany was delighted and anticipated what the future held for her and James. It was now the last day of their fasting and on that sunny spring evening of 2016 the leaves were eager to provide shade as they began sprouting on the trees. Steph just finished cleaning the entire house and relaxed on the steps. Her favorite song, "Sex Aint better than Love" by Trey Songz begins to play just as James arrived from work and sits on the steps hugging and kissing her. The good lord heard their prayers, he saw the hard work that Steph and James put in to make their marriage work. When others laughed at them for thinking outside the box, the good lord was taking note and busy doubling their blessings for all that they requested. Steph had made a nice hot bath with rose peddles, and cooked a delicious candle light lamb over rice dinner. Everything was sensational. There wasn't any nervousness from James as his mental hindrance was expelled. Later that evening after dinner, a bubble bath chaperoned their four play. She gently washed his chest as their love making carried on into the bedroom. James performed like a thorough bread racing for the triple crown. When he reduced his thrust to slow and intense she clutched his buttocks to intensify her squirting orgasm as he also exploded with excitement.

Them climaxing together was magical. Afterwards, they just cuddled with him rubbing her back. Round two was interrupted when baby Zena cried out for some attention but after she was fed it was

Stephany's appetite that increased in wanting more of James's new found self. Round two, three, and four was extraordinary. Wow, James was on a roll. She looked at him in disbelief when she tried to catch her breath and he wanted to continue without an intermission. The next morning his hormones are raging and he interrupts Stephany's routine of feeding the baby. She declines but mentions that his clothes are neatly pressed and his breakfast was made but none of that mattered. He wants sex. James had the feeling of uncontrollable superpowers. The minute he arrived home from work, sex, before going to bed, sex, on the weekends it was sex, instead of having fun with his daughter and enjoying his entire family, it was sex. There were times when he could care less if the child was clean and fed, it was all about tearing Stephany's head off. Ironically, his performance was amazing but Stephany became overwhelmed and her stamina had dramatically decreased. As the baby's awareness skills were starting to develop Steph was highly concerned about having sex with James while the baby was still in bed with them. After bringing it to his attention he answered, "First of all our daughter is a few months old now. She should be sleeping by herself. That's the reason why I spent four hundred dollars on her crib so we all could get a good night's sleep. Why the hell is she sleeping in the middle of us at night?" "Because she's still young James." "No, it's because you're spoiling her, so if you're going to have her on a sleep schedule, you should train her how to sleep by herself and stop causing problems in our relationship." "I just don't think it's right for us to be having sex in front of our child, it could be emotionally harmful." "Ok well tomorrow I'll see if I can get my money back on the crib. And I'll be honest, yes sometimes I don't want the baby around, I just want to be in bed relaxing with you. But now it just seems pointless to have such a beautiful nursery that's not being used because of stupidity."

"Your insults aren't necessary; I'm just concerned about the safety of our child." "It's stupidity like I said because the solution to the problem was already taken care of WHEN WE BUILT THE NURSERY. That's were babies sleep. Don't you think Zena would have a problem if I slept in her crib?" "I don't know, why don't you go ahead and try." "Look I don't want the baby sleeping in the middle of us at night. What if one of us accidentally rolls over and crush her?" "Ok I get your point. She'll eventually cry herself to sleep." "Not a problem." While having lunch Stephany constantly complained to her girlfriends. "I can't believe it. It's like he turned into a ferocious sex maniac. I certainly was not expecting this after fasting." "Wow" Marcy said, "So now you're complaining about having too much sex. Your stories could really drive a person into alcoholism, bar tender shot please." LOL! "Marcy its twelve thirty in the afternoon but yeah I'll have one of those," Janet mentioned and continued, "Well this is new for him, or perhaps for the both of you and he's excited. It's all about moderation. You created this monster, now tame it." "You're right Janet, it just feels like I have another job now, and it's not fun anymore." "You know what that's called?" Janet asked. "What?" "That's called being married. It's not supposed to be fun all of the time." "Yeah, and you better be glad he's not using his new powers on someone else after all that work you've put in, trying to get him to be the man you want." "Yup" Janet agreed. "And those female prescription medications or over the counter enhancement drugs are certainly not needed. It's all about HONEST COMMUNICATION." Janet commanded.

Steph tried to issue that honest communication but it led to a dispute with James disagreeing. "My whole entire life people always told me to get on the ball, now that I'm on the ball, you're telling me to slow my roll. This is very confusing." "I'm saying it's great, but just as we found other ways to maneuver the bad sex, we can find or continue doing other things so the great sex won't get corny." She explained. He disagreed again. "No, it's either you get the steam rolling locomotive sex or I'll go back to the old James." "You're being absolutely ridiculous." "No, you're being ridiculous, now that the tables have turned maybe it's you that need to step up your game. Do you know how many women would love to have your problem?" "This is not how I envisioned this conversation." "Are you kidding me? I can't believe we're even having this discussion." James then turns up the heat. "I see you didn't complain about having too much sex with Roy's ugly ass. Now you want me to calm down. Well I guess we won't be having sex anymore, because every time we do, I'm going to TURN-UP and SHOW OUT! Wooooo!! Then he strolled out of the room like George Jefferson. Hahaha. But James was just being a jerk. He knew that Steph was right but also knew that he had went too far by mentioning Roy. So it was now time to reach into his bag of tricks. The next evening as she was busy putting the baby to sleep, James turned off all of the lights and created a candle lit heart on the floor and placed a chair in the middle. It was so romantic.

They carefully stepped over the candles, he sat her down, massaged her shoulders and washed her feet in a pail. But there was no intercourse. He then spoke softly. "I know that you're tired, you've been working twice as hard now for the past few weeks but I still wanted to please you in other ways. It's all about moderation and balance." He then gave her a piece of chocolate cake with whip cream with a cherry on top. They just sat in the middle of the heart together rand relaxed while listening to some music. James had made some changes, drastically would be more appropriate but it was time for Stephany to make some adjustments as well. After visiting her parents, she and her mother reminisced about her childhood days playing the violin. Steph's first place trophies weren't wrapped up in the attic they remained freshly polished on the mantel. Her mother regrettably admitted, "Your father and I are getting tired of the city life. We're both going to be retiring this year."

"Mom, I think it would be a great idea if you guys came to live closer to us." "Oh, sweetie I don't want to be a burden." "I said closer to us, not with us. Hahaha" "That would be great sweetie." A few months later James found a wonderful two-bedroom retirement home for his in-laws. The extra help with the baby was certainly an asset and with mom being closer, their pajama parties were even better. One weekend all of the ladies had another sleep over at Stephany's home. Marcy wasted no time with her antics and crazy probing. "What age did you guys begin talking to yourselves?" Hahahaha, "Oh lord, it never seems to end with this chick." Janet said. "I can recall maybe around my early twenties in college," Mrs. Williams answered. "I had numerous discussions with myself, especially before a presentation for work. This started for me around my late teens." Steph's mom confidently admitted. Everyone then sat quietly sipping their wine as Janet spoke. "After my husband George passed away I began questioning myself then answering my own questions. Then I started having disagreements then ultimately convincing myself that whatever I was thinking was true. I was losing it but having this nut right here (Marcy) as one of my best friends giving me some great laughs certainly helped. Thank you." Awww... everyone consoled Janet as Steph admitted, "I can't help but to talk to myself. Sometimes it gets so boring that I purposely try to keep the baby awake just so I'll have something to do." LOL! Steph cracked open another bottle of wine just as Marcy asked the group about a newspaper article that did a story on a mother who was thirty years old and had a sixteen-year-old daughter and two toddler boys. The mother prevented her daughter from participating in a parenting project for her school, that included carrying around a doll baby 24/7. James's mother stated, "What a fool, she was supposed to allow her daughter to attend the class, so that the same mistakes wouldn't be repeated." Janet agreed, "The classes are very helpful." Steph chimed in, "The mother was probably concerned about her daughter getting too attached to the doll baby, then really wanting to have a kid of her own." "That's true, that's true," they all agreed.

For Stephany, it felt great to have her family and friends around but a feeling of emptiness still remained. Some sort of daily entertainment was needed but of course not for the additional income. To fulfill her self-worth, Steph decided to get a DAMN JOB. LOL! So after getting the confirmation from James, "Hey maybe that wouldn't be so bad." Stephany got a part-time job playing the violin at her parent's retirement home for their event nights. Everyone came out to show support. All the ladies were beautifully dressed in their ballroom gowns and had great seats to cheer her on. "Maybe I'll get lucky and hook up with one of those old rich guys who doesn't care about sex and is just desperate for my affection," Marcy hoped. When they took a short break, James assured Mr. Williams as they both stood confidently sharp sporting tuxedos, "I just want to see the days Steph and I no longer go upstairs in our own home." Mr. Williams replied, "Son with your extraordinary determination you're well on your way." Although the violin job was a part time position, Stephany wanted to reach a broader audience and make a difference in her community by spreading the good love as much as possible. So the income that was made from the retirement home was used to opened and fund a studio providing inner city children with free violin lessons. It was an immediate success with kids lining up with their parents and the classes instantly being booked. Steph felt terrible about telling the others that the class was at full capacity but was thrilled to begin teaching her new protégés. The instructor's position was an excellent idea. She taught violin lessons three times a week which drastically invaded James's usual moments of desire. But they taught each other the perfect lesson about having balance.

CHAPTER 19

The Public

AUTHOR SELF DISCLOSURE – My inspiration for writing this book came at a very embarrassing moment before being intimate with a very beautiful young lady who I knew since childhood. I was either over eager, causing our chemistry to be unbalanced or I wasn't psychological attracted to her. But the fact of the matter is that I simply dropped the ball during this sexual encounter which resulted in my lack luster performance. She went on to say how handsome and how much of a great guy I was and that it was alright. That response was an unacceptable pity party. Over the next few days while relaxing in bed, my self-esteem remained shot but inspiration began to brew. I began to wonder was my usual thriving performance declining? But after simply comparing this incident to my number of gratifying experiences, I was certainly due for a blunder. Although blessed to see the maturing stage of my early thirties, where daily vitamins were insisted, I then pondered on the fact that I've never heard any of the greatest male R&B singers mention in their music that they also had a bad day in the bedroom. I then began contemplating this project and finally decided to title my third masterpiece BAD SEX, GOOD LOVE. Overwhelmed with enthusiasm I couldn't wait to hear the responses from the public so I released a promo question on Facebook and to no surprise the replies were astounding. I decided to add the replies as a chapter to show my appreciation which I hope was a delight to read just as much as I enjoyed writing this novella. Listed below are some of my favorite replies.

What if you met the guy of your dreams and he treated you like the Queen you are BUT his sex was absolutely atrocious and he's UNTEACHABLE? Would you,

A. Stay in the relationship and get some good love discretely?

B. Sticking it out like a Champ? OR

C. Leave and find happiness elsewhere?

Replies

"Great question Cornell. I'd like to be noble and say A, but life's about getting a certain degree of satisfaction out of each day, so I'm going with C."

"See ya later alligator.....lol" C.

"The only person who is unteachable is a person who doesn't want to try to do better. So with that being said, he doesn't completely treat you like a queen if he isn't trying to do better in the sex department. A King would try to do everything that he can to please his Queen." C.

"SUCH A LOADED QUESTION... I DON'T THINK NO ONE IS UNTEACHABLE, THERE IS ALWAYS ROOM FOR IMPROVEMENT." B.

"The only one you can change is yourself. If you put expectations of change onto him. You inevitably set yourself up for disappointment." C.

"The question is slanted. Why can't he get better? Is it a physical issue or a mental one? Cheating is not acceptable no matter what - even if TV makes you think it is. if you really love him, you stick with him. If not, you leave on good terms." B.

"Lol. I had a scenario like that years ago and they wondered why I never went down the road again with them." C.

"I met the man of my dreams, he wined and dined me, gifts, trips etc and blew my mind with attention and he was very romantic except for one thing....the worst lover I have ever had in my life...believe me ladies, a vibrator and toys does not take the place of a real man that knows how to really make real love to you. I will settle for a man that doesn't have a lot of tangible's but is compassionate and has good sex than a man with everything but is unteachable and bad sex. Not worth it for me. I experienced it...I tried to stay but only experienced frustration, misery coupled with sleepless nights." C.

"I was in this situation, until he no longer treated me like a Queen. Once he became disrespectful, it became an issue. So, as long as I'm being treated like a Queen. There's ways that he can be helped." B.

"Nothing will ever be complete....especially dealing with humans. I know what I Like and need in my sex life, if it ain't happening....I'm out. No time wasted...No harm no foul. He can be someone else's dream lover. Just not mine... so my answer ain't A, cause that's nasty, aids to the spread of DISEASE. Nor is it B...life is too short to settle and have a mangled pussy...it's C all day every day."

"Marriage is a partnership in ALL AREAS. A REAL man does whatever it takes to satisfy his woman both in the bedroom and out of the bedroom." B.

"If the intimacy isn't good then he wouldn't be the man of my dreams. LOL" C.

"Stick out like a champ. Cause at the end of the day!!!! I want to be treated like a queen. And if he's the man of my dreams I'll find a way to make the sex work. Honestly." B.

"I'm hoping the man of my life will come equipped, it's on the wish list. However, I would stick it out." B.

"I'm out if he's unteachable why stay when you gone end up either leaving or cheating anyway a waste of time." C.

"Outstanding question I'm out. I need the whole package. You just said he was unteachable. There isn't hope and It would be the same if you said he was good in bed, but a total dick. I'm still out. I need it all.

Even then, I really don't want to have to teach someone from the get go. They should have the basics down." C.

"Like who wants to stay in a relationship or marriage and something is missing. You have to have the whole package why would I stay and cheat myself unless you just looking for a jump off not in a position to do so because@ the end you still cheating yourself out of the other things that's awaiting for you...Like the question was self-explanatory." C.

"Leaving. I mean if he's unteachable then it's no point. Otherwise I'm gonna cheat." C.

"I'm staying but if I was younger I would leave." B.

"Sweetheart are you writing a book on my life lol when I think of the real answer I'll inbox you."

"I'm OUT. LOL!" C.

"Why would I give up the man of my dreams and the man who treats me like a queen just because the sex is bad? It would be just my luck that I leave, find someone else with the bomb sex, and he is a dog. Don't nobody have time for that. Now, what I do have time for, is to show the man of my dreams how I want it done. It should be fun too. As long as he has the goods, we will be fine. And nobody is unteachable when it comes to sex.
I'm sticking it out like a champ because people DO change and Sex isn't EVERYTHING to me in my relationship." B.

"Unteachable? what exactly is he not getting? it's not Rocket Science! If he can become fully aroused, we'll work it out." B.

"Ima stick it out, toys on deck, surly he can work a vibrator..." B.

"Well if he's the "Man of My Dreams", I'd stick it out because I don't believe in cheating. I'd just have to adjust...lol!" B.

"Unteachable huh? Well...if your that unhappy, then leave him. Another woman that don't know what "Good sex" is, will come and marry him. Then you just lost your crown, his riches and love... All for some good nookie..lol" B.

"I'm going to need to understand why he is unteachable. If he refuses, I'm out. But if he's willing to learn, I'm sticking it out."

"That's a tough one, Usually when a woman is treated like a queen, that's the way to her heart, if her heart is touched and she's in love, she'll stick it out. He can't be that unteachable, can he?"

"As long as he lets me use a toy. LOL!" B.

"I will stay because all I need is for him to sit still. I'm easy going." B.

"Oh this man will learn how to do me right. I don't have no problem showing him how it's done. Whatever it takes he will get it." B.

"Women Are wired differently than men.... Sex isn't the only way to be satisfied in a great relationship..." B.

"There are plenty of sexless marriages, and that can work as long as it's not loveless. I'd stay and remind him his mouth ain't broke!" B.

"I'd stay because at least you know what you have! You don't know what you might get and the grass is not always greener on the other side!" B.

"Cant be the man of my dreams if the sex is atrocious..." C.

"Sticking it out..sex is the icing on the cake never the foundation." B.

"What about you Mr. Author? Being sense you are a SCORPIO which is one if not the most highly sexual and passionate sign of the zodiac...If you met the woman of your dreams and the intimacy was terrible, would you A, B or C?

"I would leave and find happiness elsewhere."

By Cornell Richards

Printed in the United States
By Bookmasters